THE BAD PENNY

LINDSEY HUTCHINSON

B

Boldwood

First published in Great Britain in 2023 by Boldwood Books Ltd.

Cover Design by Head Design Ltd.

Cover Illustration: Shutterstock and iStock

A CIP catalogue record for this book is available from the British Library.

Paperback ISBN 978-1-80162-692-7

Large Print ISBN 978-1-80162-691-0

Hardback ISBN 978-1-80162-690-3

Ebook ISBN 978-1-80162-693-4

Kindle ISBN 978-1-80162-694-1

Audio CD ISBN 978-1-80162-685-9

MP3 CD ISBN 978-1-80162-686-6

Digital audio download ISBN 978-1-80162-689-7

Boldwood Books Ltd
23 Bowerdean Street
London SW6 3TN
www.boldwoodbooks.com

For Gail Owen, a loyal reader and a much-loved friend

1

BIRMINGHAM, 1894

The scream echoed along Erskine Street, rising above the cacophony of pedestrians' tramping feet and the rattle of cartwheels.

The piercing sound jolted twenty-year-old Jared Johnson from the reverie of enjoying his lunch of bread, cheese and ham. Twisting towards the direction of the noise from his seat on the cart, his eyes scanned the people in search of the woman whose howl came again.

A girl he guessed to be about his own age was sobbing as she tried to fend off the blows being rained down on her by an older man. The contretemps was taking place on a patch of stubby grass at the front of the old house.

Jared threw down his food, leapt from the cart and raced towards the melee, his hobnailed boots loud on the cobblestones. Skidding to a halt with a screech, he vaulted the rickety old garden gate to land squarely on both feet.

'Stop that!' he yelled, pulling the girl away from her assailant before standing in front of her like a shield.

'What the...?' the man gasped.

Jared stood six feet tall with broad shoulders, the rippling muscles in his arms visible beneath his rolled-up shirt sleeves. A shock of shining dark hair hung loose to reach his collar, and eyes so dark they appeared to be black glared.

'Bugger off and mind your own business!' growled the man who was in trousers and a vest, braces hanging loose.

'Not when I see a lady in distress. You should be ashamed of yourself for striking a poor defenceless girl,' Jared returned.

'I'll 'ave you know that's my daughter!'

'I don't care if she's the Queen of England, I cannot condone hitting a woman!' Jared subconsciously turned his body slightly to the right, his left foot forward in a solid bare-knuckle fighting stance, ready to raise his fists should the need arise.

'Go back to where you came from and leave me to deal with my wench in my own way.'

'I'm not moving until I have your assurance she will not be harmed further,' Jared said, aware of the gathering crowd in the street. He could hear the girl sobbing quietly behind him but his eyes stayed on her attacker.

'Fair enough, you have my word,' the man said with a greasy smile, his arms outstretched.

'He's lying,' the girl whispered.

'I'm afraid I don't believe you, mister,' Jared said as he raised an eyebrow.

'Give him a cockaiver,' a man's voice sailed out from the crowd, 'he's 'ad it coming.'

'A good pasting is what he deserves!' a female yelled.

'He's a bloody menace, he's always putting on that gel. She tells us often how he beats her,' an aged fellow croaked, raising his walking stick and waving it in the air.

'Hey, old 'un, watch what you'm doing with that thing,' a young man said as he ducked the swing of the cane.

Jared heard it all but still he watched the brute who had been beating his daughter. 'It would seem you are not very popular with your neighbours,' he said with a little grin.

'Clear off, the lot of yer!' the man said, throwing out his arm to point up the street.

Jared didn't flinch at the movement but kept his gaze on the other man's eyes. They would be the *tell*, the indicator of fight or flight, and Jared was ready for either.

'Look, mate, this ain't got anythin' to do with you so let's call it a day and you can be on your way,' the man muttered, tapping his hands on the sides of his trousers.

Jared drew in a deep breath through his nostrils, expanding his chest further, and exhaled long and slow.

The crowd were waiting a little impatiently to see if the confrontation might spill over into a real good punch-up.

Without turning, Jared asked, 'What's your name, miss?'

'Clarice,' came the reply.

'What a pretty name, and are you likely to be safe if I should do as your father suggests and leave?'

'No, I doubt it.'

'That's what I thought,' Jared said with a nod. 'So we find ourselves in a stand-off,' he directed his words to the father.

Jared noted the flash of anger in the man's eyes and he bunched his fists. This was not going to end well.

In a trice, the father leapt forward but Jared was ready for him. He raised his hands, the left guarding his face, and the right shot out in a jab. His knuckles caught the man on the nose and he staggered back. Cradling his battered proboscis, the man wailed as he saw the blood slipping between his fingers.

The crowd erupted in applause, shouts and jeers, loud as Clarice's father stared with disbelief at his bloody hands. With a rebel yell and head down, he charged forward, intent on causing bodily harm to the interfering stranger.

Jared saw it coming and at the very last moment he stepped aside, allowing the irate father to hurtle past him. Then he heard a sickening crunch as the man's head hit the wooden gate post.

A communal 'Owwww!' sounded from the crowd, and Jared saw the people wincing as they watched Clarice's father crumple at the knees.

Clarice whispered, 'I'll be for it now.'

'Clarice, you can't stay here, it's not safe. You have to leave – today,' Jared urged.

'Where would I go? I have no money – I have nothing!'

The crowd leaned in to listen to the conversation but all took a step back at Jared's next words. 'There must be someone who would be willing to take you in until you can find work.'

Clarice laughed but there was no mirth in it. 'You jest. Look at them.' She tilted her chin up, indicating the spectators. 'There's not one among them who would stand up to *him*!' Her finger jabbed in the direction of her groaning father. 'I'm trapped, kind stranger.'

'Jared Johnson is the name and I'm the manager at McGuire's Rag & Bone Yard, pleased to meet you, Clarice...?'

'Clarice Connaught,' she replied shyly, hardly noticing the hushed remarks from the crowd. They all knew Toby McGuire, the big Irishman who lived in Ivy Lane and was a force to be reckoned with.

'Well, Miss Connaught, would you care to take tea with me?' Jared said, hooking an arm.

Blushing to the roots of her hair, Clarice faltered but only for a moment, then she pushed her arm through his. 'I would, thank you, Mr Johnson.'

The two strode to his rag cart and he groaned as he saw that the pigeons were attacking the lunch he had left in his hurry to help. They flew off as he handed Clarice up into the driving seat. Picking up the reins, he called out, 'Walk on, Bess, my beauty.'

Clarice gave a little yelp as the cart lurched forward and held onto the side of the bench.

They could still hear the cheers as they turned the corner at the end of the street, Bess leading them to the tea shop.

'Dad is going to be very cross with me,' Clarice said.

'Oh, he'll be too worried about his aching head to be angry with you,' Jared answered with a grin.

Clarice threw back her head and laughed fit to burst, her curls bouncing and her blue eyes shining.

Jared's heart missed a beat as he looked at the dark-haired beauty, and he wondered – could this be what they called love at first sight?

2

The cart halted outside the tea shop and Jared assisted Clarice to alight. Grabbing the oat sack, he hung it over Bess's neck before turning back to the girl he had rescued.

Holding the door open for her to enter first, he followed her in and they walked to a table in the corner.

'This is lovely,' Clarice said as she looked around. The room was snug and welcoming, with tables covered in pristine white cotton cloths. Sunlight shone through the small mullioned windows, casting rainbow colours around the room. Gas lights adorned the walls for use on murkier winter days. Each table held a slim vase containing one flower and a sprig of greenery. Wooden chairs had cushions fastened to the seats and backs; chintz curtains were held aside in swathes by ties of the same material. The whole effect was very tasteful, Jared thought.

Customers chatted quietly as they enjoyed their afternoon tea. A waitress appeared, dressed in a long black dress covered with a white pinafore. Blonde hair piled up neatly was topped with a frilly cap.

'Good afternoon, what can I get for you?' she asked.

'Afternoon tea for two, please,' Jared answered.

'Certainly, sir.' The waitress smiled and strode away.

'I've never done this before,' Clarice whispered.

'Done what, been in a tea shop or out with a man you've only just met?'

'Both!' Clarice's eyes twinkled as she spoke.

The waitress appeared again with plates and cutlery wrapped in white linen napkins which she placed in front of them.

Clarice watched her go back to what she surmised was the kitchen and a moment later return with a tiered cake stand which held tiny sandwiches of salmon and cucumber, potted paste, jam, and cheese and onion. There were frangipane cakes, little cream horns and scones with butter, jam and cream.

'Ooh!' Clarice beamed as she eyed the food.

'Tea is coming right up, ma'am,' the waitress said pleasantly.

Clarice nodded, this was how she should be living her life, being called ma'am and taking afternoon tea.

Sure enough, a tray arrived with cups and saucers, teaspoons, milk jug and sugar bowl. Shortly afterwards, two small pots of tea arrived with steam escaping from the little holes in the lids.

'Enjoy,' the waitress said and sauntered off to clear a table near the window.

'I rather think we will, don't you?' Jared asked.

Clarice nodded, taking a sandwich and putting it on her plate, her eyes as big as the saucer which held her china cup. 'Look at me having tea with a complete stranger, but I was so scared of my dad giving me what for that I did rather jump at the chance.'

Jared's face was a picture of sympathy and only now did he note her thin frame; it could be that this was her natural state, but then again she could be under-nourished. 'You won't get fat on that,' he said with a grin and a nod to the sandwich.

'I was trying to be posh and wait for you,' she whispered, casting a glance around.

Jared laughed and took a sandwich. 'Let's dig in because I'm starving! Those pigeons finished off my lunch.'

They poured their tea through the silver strainers placed on the cups then set them on the plate set aside for the purpose.

Whilst they ate and drank, Jared tried to ease Clarice's nerves by telling her his story. He explained how his father, Tim, had left searching for work when he was a small boy. He'd returned after many years, having spent a stint in jail for accidently assaulting a policeman who was trying to break up a fight. In the meantime, Jared's mother had died of starvation and his sister had succumbed to sickness. He told her all about him setting himself up as a rag and bone man and how he had poached the notorious Mr McGuire's territory.

'I'll bet he didn't take that too well,' Clarice said.

'Actually he was really good about it. He gave me a job and now I'm his manager. I'm usually in the office but occasionally I like to take old Bess out on a round.'

'Luckily for me,' Clarice said a little sadly.

'Clarice, you know you can't go back there,' Jared said.

'I know, but...'

'Where's your mum?' Jared asked.

'Died years ago giving birth. The baby died as well.'

'I'm sorry to hear it,' Jared sympathised.

'There's just me and Dad now. The big *I am* John Connaught!' Clarice spat the words with disgust. 'He has a job at the brick works and spends most of his wages in the boozer. He's a nasty drunk so when he goes out at night I go to bed and lock my door.'

'It's not much of a life for you, though,' Jared said. 'Why was he hitting you?'

Clarice shrugged. 'He won't let me go out to work. I asked yet again and he got angry. I don't suppose I could get a job anyway.'

'I have to admit there's not much going in the way of employment. The bread lines are getting longer by the day,' Jared confessed.

Finishing her tea, Clarice said, 'Thank you, Jared. I suppose I'd better get back now.'

'Clarice, you can't! He'll beat you again – if he gets really angry, he could kill you!' Jared said in a harsh whisper.

'What else am I to do?' she asked, tears glistening on her dark lashes.

'I know we've only just met, but do you trust me?'

Clarice nodded at the young man who had saved her from a severe beating.

'Right, well, come with me then, I have an idea.'

Jared paid, giving the waitress a tip, then outside he removed Bess's nose bag. Clarice climbed up onto the driving seat. When he joined her, she asked, 'What do you have in mind?'

'You'll see,' Jared replied with a warm smile.

'Jared...'

'You'll have to come home with me.'

'I can't do that! People will talk.'

'They won't if you were my housekeeper. I could pay you a little if you tidied around a bit and did the shopping and suchlike. You'd be safe then away from your father.'

Resting a hand on his arm, Clarice said, 'No, Jared. I have to go back – please. It's nice of you to offer but I can't. I'd be talked about something rotten and then I'd get a reputation as a harlot.' Having tea with this man in a public place didn't mean she should go to his home. He'd been kind enough, but he could be a murderer, and worry etched her face.

'But...'

'It's for the best. I thank you for what you did for me and for the afternoon tea, but I really must return home.'

With a loud sigh, Jared nodded, he could see the determination in Clarice's blue eyes. 'All right, but only if you promise to leave if your father strikes you again.'

Clarice gave him a nod.

'You can always find me at McGuire's yard if you need help.' With that, he clucked to Bess and they travelled back to Erskine Street in worried silence.

3

Arriving back at Erskine Street, Jared climbed from the cart and helped Clarice onto the ground.

'I'm not happy about leaving you here,' he said quietly.

'I'll be all right. Dad will be at work now and I'll be in bed when he gets home,' she answered.

Jared felt himself to be on the horns of a dilemma. Should he just go and leave the girl to her fate, or should he insist that she come with him?

Clarice made the decision for him when she said, 'Thanks, Jared. Maybe I'll see you again sometime.'

'I hope so,' he said with a forced smile. He watched her enter the house before going back to his cart and hauling himself onto the driving seat. He sat there a moment to ensure there were no more sounds of argument coming from within the house, then he picked up the reins. 'Come on, Bess, I think she's safe enough for now.'

Obediently the old mare walked on and the cart rattled down the street, away from the prying eyes of the neighbours.

No longer feeling in the mood for more trading, Jared led the horse back to the yard, oblivious to the noises of the busy streets.

He was greeted at the gates by the two big burly brothers Bobby and Dicky Cavenor, who were the guardians of the yard as well as Jared's bodyguards. As the cart came to a halt, Jared called out, 'Everything all right?'

'Yes, Boss,' they chorused.

The brothers stood sentinel at the gates to deter any would-be troublemakers and had been bodyguards to Toby McGuire. Now they protected Jared with the same love and respect. They watched as the cart rolled through into the yard where it was met by the sorters.

'What's up with him being back so early?' Bobby asked.

'I dunno, but summat ain't right,' Dicky answered.

A moment later, a whistle sounded, summoning them to the office.

'P'raps we'll find out now,' Bobby said, raising his eyebrows as they strode across the yard.

Climbing the steps to the office, they knocked on the door-jamb and walked in.

'You called, Boss?' Dicky asked.

Jared nodded. 'What do you know about a bloke called John Connaught?'

'He's a nasty piece of work from all reports,' Bobby said.

'Lost his wife years ago,' Dicky added.

'He's got a daughter called... erm.' Bobby scratched his head as he searched his mind for the name.

'Clarice,' Jared provided the answer.

'Yeah, that's it,' Bobby said with a frown. 'Why are you asking about John?'

Jared held up a finger then said, 'Firstly, is there anything else you know about the man?'

'I've heard he likes a drink,' Dicky answered.

'He puts me in mind of Ned Watkins,' Bobby said.

Jared sighed. Ned Watkins was father to Seth, who shared Jared's house. He was a drunken bully who had beaten Seth half to death one night because he wanted Seth's money for beer. The money in fact had belonged to McGuire; Seth had been stealing little and often to add to his savings so he could get out from beneath the yoke of his tyrannical father. Ned had spent that money and left his son in a very sorry state. It was McGuire who had rescued Seth and taken him into his own home with help from the Cavenors. Ned Watkins had then fallen out with his best friend and, after picking a fight outside a pub, had been pushed and cracked his head on the wall. He had died even before the police arrived.

The recollection made Jared shiver as he sat behind the desk.

Bobby repeated his question, breaking Jared's thoughts. 'Why do you want to know about John, Boss?'

'I met him today and we had a bit of a to-do,' came the answer. Jared went on to explain the circumstances in which he had met Clarice and her father, and that she had insisted on going home after Jared had taken her for tea.

Now the brothers sighed. 'Oh, shit!' Bobby said eventually.

'I have a feeling history is about to repeat itself,' Jared mumbled.

'Let's hope not,' Dicky said.

'In what way?' Bobby asked.

'Ned Watkins had battered poor Seth to within an inch of his life when you and Mr McGuire rescued him, remember? I'm praying the same won't happen with John Connaught and his daughter.'

'Oh, I see what you mean now,' Bobby said sheepishly.

'Okay, thanks, both,' Jared said and watched the big men nod then leave the office to return to their posts on the gates, muttering together as they went.

Jared's mind then returned to the pretty Clarice and he knew he would be worrying about her for some time to come.

Later that afternoon, the tatters rolled in one by one and Jared stood in the yard to greet them. Here they came: Dan, Sam, Johnny, Paul, Tom and Seth – his friends.

Dan Freeman lived alone in Miles Street; he was an orphan too. Johnny Baker had flaming red hair, a twin sister and was a bit of a joker. Paul Clancy was the eldest of five children with a father unable to work because of the coal dust in his lungs. Tom Brooks, once a sorter then promoted to tatter, lived with his older sister and her husband who had taken care of him when their parents died. Sam Jenkins, mild of manner, lived in Bromley Street with his over-protective mother. Then there was Seth, Jared's housemate.

When Jared had been on the rounds, they had all formed a firm bond which continued despite his rise in status to become their manager. Jared had taken to his new role like a duck to water, making sure that home and work life were kept separate. His friends had accepted this without question, each happy to see him promoted – it was well deserved in their opinions.

They still walked home together once work was done and continued also to have an occasional card night over at Jared's. With the extra money coming in, Jared had been able to buy bits of furniture here and there so now they could all have a chair rather than having to sit on the floor. The house was nicely deco-rated and the larder kept full. He had also arranged for the night-soil men to call bi-annually to clear out the privy. Usually a team of four men with barrels on a cart would arrive at the privy to do their work. They were only allowed to work in darkness, after midnight. The hole-man would descend into the pit to await the bucket to be lowered by the rope-man. Using a long-handled dipper, the hole-man would shovel the mephitic waste into the buckets. Hauled up by the rope-man, the buckets would then be emptied into the barrels on the cart by the two tub-men. This would then be sold on to farmers for fertiliser or thrown onto a paddock called the night-soil depository. These men worked in dangerous conditions as they could easily be asphyxiated, and all for twenty-three shillings a week.

Jared had moved into the abandoned house shortly after his family had died and, dilapidated as it was, had claimed it as his own. He had lived there for five years now and no one had ever questioned his residing there.

Watching the young men jump from their carts and chat with each other and the sorters and grooms, Jared considered himself a lucky man to be blessed with such friends.

Not so for Clarice Connaught, he thought, and a sadness covered him like a shroud.

Once the carts had been emptied by the tatters and sorters working together, the horses were then led to the stables to be fed, watered and rubbed down.

A short while later, Jared locked the office and once everyone was out he secured the big gates. On the walk home, he explained about his meeting with Clarice and her father.

'Bloody hell, here we go again!' Johnny said with a grin. 'Somebody else coming to try and bash your brains out.'

'They can try,' Tim Johnson said as he caught up with the gang.

'It's possible John Connaught could cause trouble, Dad,' Jared said.

'Maybe but we stick together, eh, boys?' Tim said.

'Aye!' Everyone spoke in unison.

Parting ways, Jared and Seth strolled home in silence, each thinking the same thing – would John Connaught turn out to be another Ned Watkins?

4

John Connaught sat at the kitchen table nursing his banging head, a tea towel held against the cut on his scalp.

Clarice was surprised to find that he hadn't gone into work as she thought he would have.

'Where have you been?' he demanded to know when she walked in.

'Out!' Clarice snapped.

'Don't shout, I've got a headache,' he muttered.

'I don't doubt it,' Clarice said, eyeing the blood on her clean tea cloth.

'You shouldn't push me, Cl—'

'Oh, I knew it would be my fault, it always is,' she cut across his words.

'Look, we've had this argument many times before and—'

'We'll have it many more until you realise I'm no longer a child!'

'I am *not* having you spending time with young men like you did today, and that's that!' John yelled and then groaned as the drum beat in his head played out a steady rhythm.

'What sort of life is it for me? I have to cook, clean, wash and look after you when you come in from work every night! I have no friends and I don't see a soul from one weekend to the next!' Clarice poured her heart out, hoping her father would understand.

'You're lazy, Clarice, tell the truth and shame the devil! You should be out trying to find work, but do you? No, you spend your time spreading malicious gossip with the neighbours. You hardly lift a finger in this house, it's like a pigsty!'

'I don't want to go out to work, I like being at home!' Clarice blasted.

'So you can stand at the gate flaunting yourself like a strumpet? Oh, I've heard all about it from the neighbours. They love the gossip, Clarice. You think they feel sorry for you because your mum died? Well, they don't, they see you trying to attract any bloke who passes by.'

'I do not!' Clarice denied the accusation, all the while knowing it was true. She knew she had inherited her mother's good looks and she was aware of the effect it had on men as they walked down the street.

'I know all about the malice you spread about me as well and you should be ashamed of yourself. I've only ever tried to do right by you, and this is the thanks I get.' John's despair was evident as he shook his head.

'I'm lonely, Dad, I need company.'

'I don't think you realise, I'm lonely as well since your mother died.'

'That was down to you as well!' Clarice said spitefully. Then as she saw the devastating effect her words had on her father, she could have bitten off her tongue.

John's chin dropped to his chest, a look of pure misery on his countenance.

'I'm sorry, Dad, I didn't mean it.' Clarice tried to assuage the situation but she knew the damage was done.

'Yes, you did. You were only nine years old when your mum passed. She wanted more children and we tried for years; when she finally conceived, she was overjoyed. Then she went into labour but the baby wouldn't come. The midwife tried her best but in the end we lost the child.' John's voice cracked and a dry sob escaped his lips.

Clarice listened in silence; this was the first time John had spoken of it in the ten years since it happened.

'Dad, women die in childbirth all the time,' Clarice said quietly. 'Mum was one of the unfortunate ones.'

'If I'd been more restrained... if we hadn't kept trying, your mum wouldn't have got pregnant again.'

'Let's not go there, Dad, it's in the past now,' Clarice said, feeling uncomfortable at the personal turn in the conversation.

'True enough. Alas, it was the flu that took your mum in the end.' John nodded and winced, the pain in his temples reminding him of the incident with the tatter. 'Anyway, where did you go with that lad?'

'Jared took me for tea.'

'Jared, is it?' The question had a sharp edge to it and John saw his daughter sigh heavily.

'Jared Johnson and he's the manager at McGuire's,' Clarice explained.

'So if that's the case, why was he out on the road then?' John asked, not entirely believing her.

'He likes to go on the round occasionally and it exercises his horse.'

With a shake of his head, John scoffed, 'I doubt it. He's lying to you, girl.'

'He's not! Jared was a perfect gentleman.'

'I'm sure he was and would continue to be so until he got you into his bed.'

'Dad! I could tell Jared isn't like that and neither am I! How could you even think that?'

'Because I was young once. I'll bet you didn't know you were on the way before your mother and I were married, such was our love for each other.'

Clarice's mouth opened in complete shock as she stared at her father. This was all too much and as her tears fell, she fled from the kitchen to the safe haven of her bedroom. Locking the door and wedging a chair under the handle, she sat on her bed and cried.

How had this day become such a disaster? All she had done was say she wanted friends, but her father had called her lazy and told her she should be out working. The result had been utter chaos. Her father had beaten her out in the street... it was too awful to even think about. The only good thing to come from all this was – she had met Jared Johnson. Unfortunately, she would probably never see him again.

Drying her tears, Clarice tried to pull herself together. She was a young woman now and her dad was right, she ought to be out in the world earning a living for herself. She had finally had enough of disagreeing with her father and she determined now was a good time to stand on her own two feet. She had an exciting journey ahead of her if only she could find the courage to take the first step.

5

That same evening, after a hearty meal of meat and vegetable pie and chips with a generous helping of salt and vinegar, Jared and Seth washed their dishes and then the friends sat before a crackling fire.

Jared watched the dancing flames tumble and roll around the logs lying on a bed of glowing coals.

'You can't do anything if she doesn't want your help,' Seth said quietly, having guessed his friend's thoughts.

'I know but I'm still worried about her,' Jared replied, without taking his eyes from the fire.

'What will you do then?'

'I don't know, mate,' Jared replied.

'Why don't you sleep on it? Maybe by the morning you'll have an idea,' Seth suggested.

Jared nodded and, saying goodnight, he retired to his bed. He was tired and hoped sleep would not elude him. A little while later, he heard Seth come up the stairs to his own room, but Jared had very little rest. He tossed and turned most of the night, his thoughts on Clarice. She was a rare beauty with skin like porcelain. Her dark hair shone and her blue eyes twinkled like stars. The cadence of her voice was like rippling water and her smile lit up her whole face. Jared was surprised that there was not a line of gentlemen at her door begging for her favours.

The following morning, Jared rose early. Dressing quickly in the cold bedroom, he went downstairs to start breakfast. Rekindling the range, he put bacon in a frying pan and set it on the hotplate. Glancing out of the window, he saw a thin mist had descended during the night.

Tending the bacon, he heard Seth clomping about upstairs and a minute later the young man joined him in the warm kitchen. Bacon cooked and on a plate, Jared cracked two eggs into the pan. Serving the food, he then dipped two slices of bread in the liquor while Seth made tea.

The pair ate in a sluggish silence born of having had very little sleep.

Seth washed the dishes and Jared dried and put them away, then both donned jackets, mufflers and caps and set off for work, locking the door behind them.

The sun had risen by this time and burned off most of the mist and the air was full of the promise of a warm day ahead, but Jared knew that when the sun slipped beneath the horizon again, a chill would steal across the land.

For all his troubled thoughts, Jared could not help but notice autumn in all her beauty. Leaves of scarlet and molten gold had begun to float lazily from the trees, leaving behind vibrant green ones holding on until the last minute as they stole every drop of moisture from their host. High in the canopy, crows cawed loudly, beating their wings in dispute of the best roosts. Insects buzzed past speedily in a last desperate dash to their nests before either hibernation or death overcame them.

Jared and Seth trudged on over the grass wet with morning

dew and the remains of the mist, hands in their trouser pockets and snap tins under their arms. Neither spoke of Clarice and whether Jared had come to a decision about her. In fact, Jared had thought of nothing else but had still not come to a satisfactory conclusion. He remained unsure; he wanted to visit her to reassure himself she was all right, but he didn't want to get her into more trouble with her father. With an inward nod, he determined he would speak with his own father about the whole thing. Maybe Tim could advise him on the best way forward.

Arriving at the gates, he saw the Cavenors waiting for him to unlock the yard. 'Morning, Mr Bobby, Mr Dicky,' he said, maintaining the respect he had shown them from their first meeting.

'Mornin', Boss,' the reply came in unison.

Once the heavy padlock was unfastened, they all shoved the gates open and Jared and Seth walked into the yard, leaving the brothers at their posts.

Jared was in the office as the grooms, sorters and tatters filed in one at a time or in little groups. Another day had begun as men moved around feeding horses and sorting rags. One man whistled a little tune and before long a pleasant chorus rang out as others joined in.

Shouts of 'See you later' echoed as each cart in turn left the yard to traverse the streets in search of bundles of rags.

Jared sat brooding behind the large desk, his mind again on Clarice Connaught. Getting to his feet, he went to the door and yelled, 'Dad, can you spare me a minute, please?' He saw the other sorters glance at Tim as he nodded. They would be curious and want to know what was going on.

Tim ran up the steps, knocked on the open door and strode in, affording his son the respect of being the manager.

'I need some advice, Dad,' Jared said, pointing to a chair. As Tim sat, Jared explained his dilemma.

Eventually Tim said, 'If you're that concerned, why not visit her? Her father will most likely be at work, so you'll be safe enough.'

'I'm not scared for myself, Dad, I'm frightened for her.'

'Maybe a little enamoured too?' Jared blushed, his cheeks aflame. 'I thought so,' Tim added.

'If John Connaught finds out I've been to the house again, he could get angry and take it out on Clarice!'

'I see your problem but if you don't go – you'll never know,' Tim said wisely.

'P'raps I should let sleeping dogs lie—' Jared began.

'And spend the week in a constant state of worry?' Tim interrupted.

The two eyed each other across the desk, both thinking the same thing – Jared *had* to visit Clarice again.

Without another word, Tim rose to go back to his work.

'Thanks, Dad,' Jared said as he too got to his feet.

Descending the steps, Tim returned to the sorters, saying loudly so Jared could hear, 'Woman troubles!'

Jared grinned as the men cheered and clapped. Making his way to the stables, he told the grooms he was going on the road for a few hours. They quickly hitched Bess to the cart and Jared climbed into the driving seat. 'Walk on,' he called which Bess duly did. Halting her by the gates, he said, 'Watch the yard for a while, please, I won't be long.'

'Yes, Boss,' Bobby said. The brothers tipped their bowler hats and Jared nodded. He noted how smart they were in their black suits and hats, shoes polished to a mirror shine, giving the business an air of respectability.

As he made his way to Erskine Street, Jared began to have misgivings. Doubts rose in his mind like monsters and more than once he almost turned back. Then an image of Clarice trying to fend off her father's blows made him determined to go on.

Feeling sure the neighbours would not report his visit to John Connaught, for clearly the man had alienated himself from them, Jared relaxed a little. He wouldn't stay long and he certainly wouldn't go into the house, he would simply ask if she was all right and then he would leave. It all sounded so easy in his head, and as the cart rattled along, he hoped it would be.

6

Entering Erskine Street, Jared drew Bess to a halt. Taking an apple from his pocket, he jumped down and walked forward. Feeding her the fruit, he said, 'Wait for me and don't wander off.' He stroked her neck, knowing the blinkers at the side of her eyes attached to the bridle would prevent her being distracted or spooked.

Vaulting the rickety broken gate which was held together with a piece of string, he walked the few steps and knocked loudly on the front door. After a moment, the door opened a fraction and a pair of blue eyes peeped out.

'Jared!'

'Hello, Clarice,' he said with a smile. 'I came to see if you were all right.'

Pulling the door open further, Clarice nodded. 'I'm fine, thank you.'

Jared sighed with relief, seeing no signs of any further abuse. 'I'm glad to hear it, I was worried.'

'I do my chores then lock myself in my bedroom when it's time for Dad to come in from work. I don't come out until he's gone the next morning,' she assured him.

'How long will he put up with that before he gets riled again, though?' Jared's words were out before he had time to think. Clarice was surprised and her eyes widened, making Jared shuffle his feet and mutter an apology.

'It's okay,' she said with a warm smile. 'I'm just being careful.'

Jared nodded, feeling awkward. In business he was strong and confident, but standing on the doorstep of a pretty young girl he felt totally lost. He wanted so much to ask her to walk out with him but was afraid she might reject him.

'Right, if you're sure you're all right...' Jared twisted the cap in his hands, having removed it when she answered his knock.

'I am and thank you for your concern,' Clarice said. She wondered if he might ask her out again, but all she could do was wait and see.

'I'd best be off then and leave you in peace,' he said, trying to straighten the mangled mess that was his cap.

Clarice nodded. Jared walked towards the gate where he stopped and turned around. The sight of her in her long brown skirt and white high-necked blouse, her dark hair shining in the weak sunshine, had his heart hammering in his chest.

Clarice gave a little wave and he raised his hand in salute before turning away and climbing over the broken gate. He strode purposefully back to Bess, who was waiting patiently. In the driving seat once more, he picked up the reins. Looking over his shoulder for one last glance at the pretty girl, his heart sank – she had gone, the front door was firmly closed.

Clucking to the mare, Jared wondered if this was Clarice's way of saying she was glad to be rid of him. He had hoped she would have stayed on the doorstep to wave him off; if she had he would have taken it as a sign that she was interested in him.

Travelling back to the yard, he was full of mixed emotions.

Happy that Clarice was fit and well and had not suffered as a consequence of his actions, but he was also sad because it was unlikely he would see her again.

Even stopping here and there to exchange bundles for pennies, the job he loved, didn't seem to lift his mood.

Hearing music coming his way, Jared pulled the cart over to watch the town band march past. At its head strode the Drum Major, twirling his long baton, which was topped with a silver ball.

'Steady, girl,' Jared said to Bess, who snickered and pawed the cobbles.

As the band passed him, Jared recalled how his sister Masie, dead these long years, used to laugh and jump up and down as she watched the procession of men dressed in their smart uniforms. His heart felt the stab of pain at her loss and that of his mother when he was but twelve years old.

He watched as mothers came out of their houses to clap along with the melodies and children squealed with delight as they puffed out their little chests, swung their arms and stamped their feet alongside the musicians.

The steady rhythmic beat of drums and marching feet fading, Jared urged Bess onwards.

Arriving back at the yard, Jared acknowledged the nods of the Cavenors at the gate before proceeding into the yard proper. Jumping down, he unhitched Bess and walked to the stables, the horse following sedately. The grooms rubbed her down while Jared plodded his way back across the yard, and gave a nod to his father who had raised his eyebrows in question as to how things had gone with Clarice.

Running up the steps to the office, Jared dropped into the big chair behind his desk. Gathering the ledgers together ready for his weekly meeting with Toby McGuire, Jared tried his best to shake the despondent feeling which had settled on him. The quietness in the yard told him it was lunchtime but Jared had no appetite. He heard the buzz of conversation as the sorters and grooms exchanged gossip while they consumed whatever food they had brought with them.

Jared propped his elbow on the arm of the chair and rested his cheek on his knuckles with a sigh. He decided this would be where he would stay until Toby arrived to check the books.

7

Whilst Jared was moping in his office, Clarice sat in the kitchen doing much the same thing. She had really hoped Jared Johnson might have asked her out for afternoon tea again but he had not. Clearly he was concerned for her welfare, as could be seen by him jumping in and saving her from her father's wrath. Then he had taken the time to call upon her to ask after her well-being, but that was all it was – a friendly visit. He had given her no indication that it could be any more than that. Clarice shook her head and sighed deeply as she saw an image of the handsome young man in her mind.

Clarice spent her days looking after her father and now at nineteen years old she had still not had the opportunity to meet a prospective husband. She feared she would die an old maid, never having experienced wedded bliss or raising a family of her own. By the time her father passed on, she would be too old to attract a life partner.

I'm not asking for the moon, she thought, all I want is someone who will take care of me without trying to batter me to death! Someone with money, of course, so I don't have to do these bloody chores. Clarice looked around her at the dirty kitchen, dishes piled high in the sink and bits of food scattered on the tiled floor. What I'd like is a maid, cook and a big house; none of which I would get with Jared Johnson. I suspect he has a little money put by, but not nearly enough to satisfy me.

The lid on the old kettle began to clatter as the hiss of steam escaped. Grabbing the cloth, Clarice got to her feet and removed the kettle from the range hotplate. Pouring boiling water over the tealeaves in the pot, she replaced the kettle on the range but between the hotplates. Dropping the small lid on the teapot, she sat down once more, laying the cloth on her lap. Looking at the cheese and bread on the plate, she curled her lip and pushed it away from her. She didn't want food, she wanted a man of means.

Since the death of her mother, Clarice had felt very lonely. Her father had withdrawn into himself and subsequently was in no fit state to raise a daughter. Clarice had virtually grown up on her own, having to deal with the trauma of the onset of her monthlies by herself. She had stepped into the role of carer very young; she learned to cook by trial and error but was now very proficient at it, not that she did much if she could get away with it.

Pouring the tea, now stewed, she drank without tasting it as she stared out of the kitchen window. Jared was right that this was no life for a girl of her age, but what could she do about it? At least here she had a warm bed and food in her belly, but if she left she would have nothing.

With a sniff, she knew she had to accept her lot, like it or not.

Standing up once more, she put a small piece of string beef to boil, then she peeled and chopped some carrots and potatoes to go into the broth she was preparing. Once the meat was cooked and the water cooled, she would scrape off the fat into a cup; this dripping could then be spread onto a chunk of bread and sprinkled with salt and pepper. When the food was ready, she would have hers and then lock herself in her room, her father could have his meal when he came in.

Suddenly the enormity of her situation hit her like a steam train; her meeting a young man for the first time in her life and then watching him walk away from her. Being a skivvy in the hovel she lived in; having to do the housework every day and being paid nothing for her efforts. Slumping into a kitchen chair, Clarice Connaught could not prevent the paroxysm of tears which overwhelmed her and she cried like her heart was breaking.

* * *

Simultaneously, over at the yard, Jared was deep in thought about how he could find an excuse to visit Clarice again. Of course he could just stride up to the house and ask her out, but the image of the closed door as he had left her rose in his mind, taunting him. If she wanted him, wouldn't she have waited and waved to him again? Then there was her father to consider. Jared was certain John Connaught would not allow his daughter to walk out with the young man who had bloodied his nose and made him look a fool in front of his neighbours.

The sonorous tones of Toby McGuire's voice broke Jared's train of thought and he got to his feet and strode to the doorway.

Toby was laughing with the Cavenors and shaking their hands. Jared looked the big Irishman over, dressed in a smart dark suit and bowler hat. Toby had missed the chance of proposing to the love of his life, wanting to first build up his business of the tatter's yard. She had then married another and had twin sons who had married sisters who ruled their lives with iron fists. Alice Crawford had instead been Toby's housekeeper for many years and all through her married life. Then, five years ago, she had become a widow. It transpired that she and Toby had both loved each other since their school days so, very soon after burying her husband, she and Toby had wed at last.

Jared smiled warmly when Toby climbed the steps to the office.

'Ah, Jared my boy, the top of the morning to you.'

'Hello, Mr McGuire, come on in. Everything is ready for you,' Jared answered, indicating the ledgers on the desk.

Toby nodded as he sat. 'I can't deny I've missed this,' he said as he tapped his hands on the arms of the chair.

'I can imagine, you were here for many years.'

Toby glanced up at the young man who he had promoted to manage his beloved business and he frowned. The two had become close over the years and Toby could see Jared was not his usual jovial self. Leaning back in the chair, he said, 'Ah now, I see that something's troubling you.'

Jared shook his head. 'It's nothing to do with the business. All is fine there, actually, it's doing really rather well as you'll see from the books.'

Toby pointed to the other chair and watched as Jared sat. 'Tell me,' he said simply.

Taking a deep breath, Jared then launched into the tale of Clarice and her father.

When he had finished, Toby sighed. 'That *jackeen*!' Seeing Jared's frown, he explained, 'It means obnoxious man. So what do you intend to do about Clarice?'

'There's nothing I can do.'

'As I see it, there are two options. You can forget all about her and that rat of a father, or you can go and declare your feelings to her, for I know you have them, so I do.'

Jared blushed, saying, 'What if she doesn't feel the same?'

'Well now, at least you'll know.'

Jared nodded at the wisdom of his employer's words.

'Look, Jared, I waited all my life for Alice. Don't you make the same mistake – please!'

'Yes, Boss,' Jared said with a crooked smile.

Toby's laughter boomed out before he opened one of the ledgers. 'To business,' he said.

Satisfied that all was indeed good with the tatting, Toby stood to leave. 'Don't forget what I said about young Clarice. Go and see her and put your mind at rest.'

'Thanks, Mr McGuire,' Jared replied, still feeling unsure as to whether it was the right thing to do. He desperately wanted to, he just needed to find the courage.

Toby left his manager and his yard and strode home to Ivy Lane. Once indoors, he called out, 'I'm home, *mavourneen*.'

'I'm in the kitchen,' Alice returned.

Walking towards the voice, Toby halted in the doorway. He slid his eyes over his wife, who had her back to him, and his heart melted. She had retained her slim figure over the years and her hair now held touches of grey here and there.

She turned and gave him a beaming smile and Toby could not resist. With a few steps he was at her side, his arms wrapped around her. He kissed her lovingly before she pushed him away playfully.

'Everything all right at the yard?' she asked.

'It is indeed, but young Jared is in love,' he answered.

'Oh, who is the girl, do we know her?' Alice asked as she placed a steaming teapot on the table.

'Clarice Connaught.'

Alice's eyes shot up from the cup she was filling. 'John Connaught's girl?'

'The very same,' Toby said, taking the cup held out to him.

'Bloody hell, Toby!' Alice gasped as they both sat at the table.

'My thoughts exactly.'

Alice sighed deeply. 'Christ, Toby, first Ned Watkins and now that bleeder, Connaught! Those lads attract trouble.'

Toby nodded then sipped his tea.

'So what will Jared do now?' Alice asked, once Toby had filled her in on the way Jared had met Clarice.

'Both Tim and I suggested he go and see the girl; it might be she feels the same, then he can take it from there.'

'You're encouraging him, you bugger! What if John Connaught finds out?'

'Sure, he's bound to eventually, but Jared has some good pals around him and there's always the Cavenors,' Toby replied with a grin.

'I don't like it, that lad could find himself neck deep in the shit!'

'Ah now, don't you be worrying about Jared, he can take care of himself, so he can.'

With another sigh and a shake of her head, Alice dropped her eyes to her teacup.

'Sweetheart, I'll watch out for him as well,' Toby reassured her.

Lifting her eyes to him, Alice smiled. 'Just you be sure to keep him safe.'

Toby patted her hand which lay on the table beside her cup,

knowing his words would ease her mind. 'Now, *colleen*, what's for my dinner?'

'Always thinking of your stomach, ain't you? Mince and taters and apple cake for afters.'

'May the most you wish for be the least you get,' Toby said, rubbing his hands together.

'There you go again with your bloody Irish sayings,' Alice said with a laugh. 'Bugger off out of my way while I get started.'

With a kiss, Toby retired to the living room to think on what Jared had told him and whether Clarice Connaught might well have feelings for the lad. Part of him hoped not, as although it would make Jared unhappy, it would be for the best all round. However, if she was carrying a candle for him, then it could be as Alice had pointed out, Jared would find himself in a big pile of shit.

John Connaught was a widower, and people believed he was a drunk and a bully, but Toby couldn't state this as a fact. He was about Toby's age and although they had not grown up together, John's reputation had preceded him. He had few, if any, friends that Toby could ascertain and he treated his daughter like a slave. He had really gone off the rails after burying his wife and newborn son, taking his drinking to a whole new level, so it was said.

Toby allowed his thoughts to take a step further; what if Jared and Clarice were to try to marry? John would cause a stink about that for a start, then he could try to prevent the wedding taking place, though quite how he would do that eluded Toby for the moment. If, by some miracle, they did wed then Clarice would move in with Jared. What then would happen to Seth, who shared Jared's house? Seth would insist on moving out but where would he go? He could go to his mother's in Dudley, but that would mean giving up his job as a tatter.

Toby puffed out his cheeks, shaking his head. The whole thing could very well be an utter mess if they weren't careful. Bringing his thoughts back to the present, he knew all that could be done for now was to wait and see what the wind blew in. Whatever it was, Toby would be on hand to help in any way he could.

In the kitchen, Alice's mind had travelled a similar path and she had reached the same conclusion. They would all have to wait and see.

Early the following morning, sitting in the office, Jared thought on Toby's advice once more. He had pondered it throughout the night and having made up his mind, he slapped his cap on his head, descended the steps and strode to the stables. With Bess attached to the cart, he walked her to the gates.

'I won't be long,' he said to the Cavenors before Bess set off at a pace.

Reaching Erskine Street once again, Jared pulled the reins gently to stop the mare. Jumping down, he walked to Clarice's house and hammered on the door.

'She ain't in,' came a voice to his left. Jared eyed the neighbour, her hair wrapped in an old rag fashioned to look like a turban and a dirty apron covering her tattered dress.

'Oh, I'll come back later then,' Jared replied.

'Won't do you no good,' the woman said, folding her arms beneath her bosom.

'Why not?' Jared asked with a frown.

''Cos she's gone.'

'Gone where?'

'How the bloody hell should I know?' the woman said curtly.

'Then how do you know she's gone?' Jared asked, feeling exasperated.

'She packed a bag and buggered off just after that varmint left for work,' the woman said.

Jared was crestfallen. Thanking the woman, he returned to his cart. All the way back to the yard, he berated himself for not declaring his feelings when he'd had the chance. Now it was too late; Clarice had left and he had no idea where she could be or where she was headed.

He began to wonder if, like Toby McGuire, he would end up waiting a lifetime before he would be married.

9

Clarice had taken what housekeeping money there was, packed a bag and left the house. Now she sat in a room in a small boarding house, wondering if she'd done the right thing. She knew that to get on in life she had to leave and, grabbing her courage in both hands, she had done precisely that. Staying at home would not give her a life of her own. Only stepping out into the big wide world would do that, but now she had she had no idea what to do next. She would need money to survive, so finding a job was paramount. She had paid for one week at the boarding house which had taken almost all of her money. To replenish her finances, she *had* to find work – or a wealthy suitor. The thought made her smile but the more she considered the idea, the brighter the notion became.

To work for a living would be hard with long hours and she would be exhausted at the end of the day. However, if she could find herself a nice gentleman who was looking for a *companion*... She nodded her head, this was definitely the way forward.

Her thoughts then drifted to Jared Johnson, her handsome saviour, and she sighed. It would have been nice to have had him as her friend, but he was no toff. He would have looked after her for sure, but Clarice now knew she wanted more. In fact, she wanted it all; trips to the theatre, dining out at posh venues, furs, jewellery and money – lots of money. As nice as Jared was, Clarice decided he was not in a position to provide all these things for her. No, she had to push the young man from her mind and concentrate on bagging herself a true gentleman. The only question was: how to go about it?

As evening descended, Clarice had a sudden thought. Pulling out her mother's clothes she had kept for so long and had taken with her when she left home, she donned a red woollen dress, black jacket and with hat, shoes and bag to match, she set off for the theatre. Walking with a purpose, she ignored the drunks pouring out of the pubs to stagger away home.

Coming into Corporation Street, Clarice stood outside the Grand Theatre searching in her bag but with one eye on the people arriving for the performance. As two men stepped from a carriage, Clarice let out a groan and began to look around on the ground.

'Are you all right, m'dear?' one man asked.

'I appear to have lost my ticket and I so wanted to see the show,' Clarice wailed.

'That's bad luck,' the man replied.

His friend called out, 'Clifford, be a sport and buy the lady another ticket!'

'Of course. Please come inside with us,' the man named Clifford responded.

'That's very kind of you,' Clarice said as she plastered an enticing smile on her face.

'My pleasure, Miss...?'

'Christian – Clara.' Clarice's brain worked furiously to find a name she thought suitable for a middle-class lady and, more to the point, one she could remember.

'After you, Clara,' Clifford said, holding out an arm to lead her through the door held open by a doorman dressed in a fancy uniform.

'Thank you, Mr...?'

'Clifford St John, and I'm *very* pleased to make your acquaintance. This scoundrel is Anthony Purcell.'

After nodding a greeting, Clifford's friend rolled his eyes as he followed the pair into the foyer.

Once a ticket had been bought for her, she was invited to share their box, and Clarice felt a little thrill as she accepted the kind offer. Seated in the box high up on the wall of the theatre, Clarice gazed around her. Gas lighting illuminated the vast room and down below were the cheaper seats. The orchestra pit was slowly filling with musicians who immediately began to tune their instruments.

Clarice was delighted when a bottle of champagne and three glasses were ordered and delivered and she giggled when the cork went pop. A dish of strawberries sat on the tray too, and glancing at them, she wondered how on earth they had managed to get them as the growing season was long gone.

'Do help yourself, Clara,' Clifford said as he noticed her eyeing the fruit.

'Thank you,' Clarice replied with yet another beaming smile as she took a strawberry delicately between her fingers. Staring at Clifford, she took the tiniest bite and closed her eyes in ecstasy. She was out to disarm this man and this was the only way she knew to do it. When she opened her eyes, she saw Clifford staring lasciviously at her.

The lights dimmed and the orchestra struck up with a rousing tune. Clarice settled back to watch the performance and only now realised she had no idea what it would be. With an inward shrug, she sipped her drink. It didn't matter because Clarice Connaught was on her way up the social ladder at last.

Having enjoyed the performance, Clarice left the theatre with the two men. In the street, she gushed her thanks for the kindness shown to her and turned to leave.

'Miss Christian, please won't you join us for dinner?' Clifford asked. He had been smitten with this lady from the moment he saw her and certainly didn't want to let her go just yet. He wanted to get to know her a little more.

Clarice lifted a gloved hand to cover her mouth in a coquettish manner and pretended to think over the invitation. 'I'm not sure...'

'Please say you will,' he said imploringly.

'All right then, thank you,' Clarice relented. 'I am rather hungry.'

'I must be on my way, Clifford, but I'll see you at the club tomorrow. Miss Christian.' Anthony Purcell nodded and walked away.

'Oh dear, I seem to have chased your friend away,' Clarice said.

'No, m'dear, Anthony will be off to the casino, so don't concern yourself.' With that, Clifford cupped Clarice's elbow and led her down the street, chatting as they went.

Clifford St John was greeted warmly by the maître d'hôtel at the restaurant who then showed them to a candle-lit table in the corner. Menus were brought and wine chosen and poured.

Clarice studied the card in her hand and her heart raced. She tried to make out the words but her reading skills were woefully inadequate. How could she choose when she couldn't read? Lifting her eyes to the dark-haired man opposite her, she whispered, 'What would you recommend?'

'The lamb shank is very good here, as is the beef dinner,' he replied.

'Then I shall have the beef,' Clarice said with a sultry smile. Having navigated the hurdle of her illiteracy, Clarice settled into easy conversation with Clifford, always keeping their talks centred on him. She watched as Clifford sniffed then tasted the wine delivered by the wine waiter. At his nod, the waiter rounded the table to pour for Clarice first then returned to top up Clifford's glass.

A short while later, the food arrived and Clarice inwardly shuddered as she glanced at the cutlery. Knives, forks and spoons were laid out and she had no idea which to use. Leaning forward, she inhaled the aroma of the beef dinner then picked up her glass and sipped her wine as she watched Clifford to see which utensils he picked up. With a little smile, she did the same and suddenly realised she had learned something new; something to stand her in good stead. They chatted as they ate, Clarice still being very careful what she said. She had invented a new persona and as such had to make sure to remember everything she told him about herself. A liar had to have an exceptional memory, after all.

The evening progressed splendidly and Clarice was eventually escorted back to the Midland Hotel, where she had told her paramour she was living.

'May I take you to dinner again tomorrow night, Clara?' Clifford asked, praying she would say yes.

'I barely know you...' Clarice began under a pretence of shyness.

'Please say you will come out with me, please!' Clifford felt besotted with the woman he had only just met and was desperate to see her again.

'Dinner then,' Clarice relented. She didn't hold out too long in case he changed his mind and left her standing.

They arranged to meet the following evening at seven o'clock and, after kissing her gloved hand, Clifford watched her into the building before the cabbie took him home.

Clarice saw the cab roll away then she slipped quietly out of the door and away into the night.

10

As Jared prepared to lock up the following evening, Bobby
Cavenor knocked on the office door jamb. 'You've got a visitor,
Boss.' Stepping aside, he ushered in John Connaught, closely
followed by Dicky.

'Mr Connaught,' Jared said, a surprised look on his face.

'John.' The man extended a hand and immediately the
brothers strode forward. Raising his hands in surrender, John
said, 'Take it easy, boys, I come in peace.'

At a nod from Jared, the brothers melted back into the
shadows by the door where they stood on guard quietly.

'What can I do for you, John?' Jared said, indicating the man
should take a seat.

'I'm not here to cause trouble, so let's get that straight from
the start. I just want to know if my daughter is with you.'

Jared kept his shock well hidden, a trick he'd learned from
Toby McGuire. His mind whirled; he had encouraged Clarice to
leave home if she became afraid. Clearly she had done so, but
did this mean her father had beaten her again?

'No, John, she's not with me.' Jared noted the worry deepen

in Connaught's eyes, the bags beneath them well on their way to resembling suitcases. 'I take it Clarice has gone then?' John nodded. 'Forgive my saying, but is it any wonder? I mean, the first time I met you, you were trying to pummel the life out of her.'

'For the first time in my life, I lost control of my temper with her,' John said sadly. 'She got to you too, didn't she?'

'I'm not sure what you're referring to,' Jared answered.

Drawing a breath John said, 'Let me tell you about Clarice, shall I?'

Jared leaned back in his chair, intrigued to hear what his visitor had to say.

'That day you and I met, if you can call it that, Clarice and I had argued about her going out to work.'

'She told me that when we had afternoon tea,' Jared confirmed.

'Let me guess, she said I wouldn't let her find a job – right?' Jared nodded. 'Well, in fact it was precisely the opposite. I've been at her for months to try to find work but she flatly refuses. She's nineteen years old and should be earning a living now so she can take care of herself.'

'Why would she tell me—?' Jared began.

'To garner sympathy! My daughter, Jared, is an inveterate liar. She's lazy and selfish. I suppose it's my fault for not reining her in before, but she went off the rails when her mother died of the influenza some years ago.'

Jared blew out his cheeks, then said, 'Clarice said your wife died in childbirth.'

'After having Clarice, my Jenny lost a baby and couldn't have any more children. There were some complications. Then she got very ill when the flu ravaged the town and she succumbed soon after.'

'I'm sorry for your loss,' Jared said quietly.

'What else did Clarice tell you, Jared? Please, let's clear the air between us.'

Jared then related how he was told John Connaught was a drunk and he beat Clarice often so she had to hide from him.

John laughed but there was no mirth in it. 'When you saw us that day – it was the first time I have ever raised a hand to that girl. We argue a lot, but until then I had never struck her. Also I'm teetotal, Jared, I don't drink – ever. I go to the pub every night to collect a jug of ale for the old lady next door. She's a cripple and can't get out any more but she loves her beer.'

'You have a bit of a reputation for fighting, I hear,' Jared interjected.

'Lies put out by Clarice. Having a swing at you was the first time I've done that in my life, hence the mess I made of it. I was so riled up and then you came along and it all went to hell.'

'You're not very popular with your neighbours, John, I saw that for myself.'

'That's because they believe the rumours circulated by Clarice while I'm at work!'

'I don't know what to think – you say one thing and Clarice says another. However, please understand when I tell you she's not with me.'

'Thank you, that's all I needed to hear. Now I have to try and find her, although God knows she could be anywhere.'

The two men shook hands across the desk before John Connaught strode from the office, leaving Jared rubbing the bristles on his chin, deep in thought.

The brothers, who had escorted John from the premises, returned a moment later.

'What do you make of that?' Jared asked.

'Well, I can't say I've ever seen him drunk,' Bobby said.

'Or fighting,' Dicky added.

'So his bad reputation was all hearsay?'

'It looks like it, Boss,' Bobby said.

Jared rubbed his tired eyes, saying, 'Thanks, both. Let's get off home and leave the Connaughts to sort themselves out.'

As he walked home with his father and his friends, Jared filled them in on John Connaught's visit.

'I know you liked her, mate, but it sounds like you're better off out of it,' Johnny said in his own inimitable way.

'Johnny!' Dan snapped, ever aware of Jared's feelings.

'What? I was only saying what you're all thinking.'

'You are probably right,' Jared said but still his heart gave a little flutter as he thought of Clarice once more.

After going their separate ways from their friends, Jared and Seth walked home in silence. They prepared and ate their meal with few words spoken and eventually, sitting before the fire, Seth said, 'You want to talk about it?'

'I can't make head nor tail of the situation, Seth. I don't know who is telling the truth.'

'Neither can I, but at the end of the day it doesn't really matter because she's out of your life now.'

'That's true. I can't help wondering where she is, though, and if she did lie to me – why?'

'You have to let it go, Jared, 'cos if you don't it will eat away at you,' Seth said gently.

A banging on the door had Jared on his feet. He'd completely forgotten it was cards night.

The lads poured in, excitedly chatting about who would win tonight.

'Oh, bugger!' Jared said.

'Eloquently put,' Seth laughed.

11

Clarice spent the day titivating herself and deciding on what to wear for her evening out with Clifford St John. With so few clothes of her own and only a few of her mother's, she had to find ways of making them look like a different outfit each time. A shawl over her jacket across her shoulder and tied beneath one arm would give a nice effect. Sitting on her bed and staring at the garments scattered around her, Clarice guessed she and Clifford would be dining out, which was all well and good, but hard cash it was not. For her to remain in the boarding house she needed money, but how to get her hands on some evaded her. She had to find a way to part Clifford from the contents of his coffers – and soon.

Glancing around the room, Clarice knew she was only here for the week, then she would be out on the street, so she had to use her time wisely. Rubbing her temples to ward off the impending headache, which was making her brain hurt, Clarice sighed heavily.

'I need money but how do I convince you to give me some, Mr Clifford St John?' she whispered.

Like a bolt out of the blue, the answer hit her and a sly smile drew the corners of her mouth upwards. Now all she had to do was decide on what to wear.

That evening, Clarice left the boarding house early and walked swiftly to the Midland Hotel, where she waited outside patiently. She went over her story in her mind again, willing it to her memory.

Before long, a cab pulled up and out stepped Clifford, dressed in a dark double-breasted Chesterfield coat with a velvet collar and sporting a top hat.

'Ah, m'dear, have you been waiting long?' he said by way of a greeting.

'No, Clifford, a moment only,' Clarice lied.

'My apologies for my tardiness.' Clifford helped her into the cab and called out an address to the cabbie.

'You look beautiful, Clara,' Clifford said as his eyes rolled over her in the dim light coming through the window from the gas street lights.

'Thank you,' came the answer on a breath. 'Where are we going?'

'Dinner first and then to a little place I know,' he replied.

Clarice forced a smile but her mind sounded a warning bell. He could be taking her anywhere; he could try to hurt her – murder her even! After all, she'd only just met him. She tried but failed to suppress a shiver at the thought.

'Are you cold, m'dear?' Clifford asked all of a sudden.

'A little,' Clarice replied.

'A warmer coat might have been more prudent, although you look ravishing in the one you have on.'

'Indeed, but I find myself...' Clarice faltered. Now was the perfect time to execute her plan. She dabbed her nose with a handkerchief she pulled from her drawstring bag.

'Go on,' Clifford encouraged.

'I am unable to purchase one until Daddy's cheque arrives,' she sniffed.

'Oh, I see. I didn't mean to upset you, Clara, please forgive my thoughtlessness.'

'That's all right, you weren't to know.' Clarice tried her best to adopt a finer speaking voice more in keeping with the upper echelons of society. She'd heard how fine ladies had spoken to their maids when she was out in the town to do her shopping at the market, and she had spent many hours trying to imitate them and endeavouring to lose her Black Country accent. 'My allowance was late last month and so far this month's has not yet reached me.'

'Ah, how beastly.'

Again Clarice dabbed her nose. This was proving harder work than she had anticipated. It was like drawing blood from a stone. Was Clifford being deliberately obtuse, or was he really a little slow on the uptake?

The carriage drew to a halt outside a smart hotel and Clifford climbed out and extended his hand to Clarice. Paying the cabbie, he hooked his arm and led Clarice inside the hotel and on towards the restaurant, proud of the beautiful woman on his arm.

Clifford helped her to remove her coat and shawl before checking them into the cloakroom along with his own coat and his hat. Then they were shown to a table that was covered in cutlery and glassware.

Clarice felt panic rise in her chest at again being expected to read and choose from the menu. A waiter arrived and filled their glasses with water from the carafe which he replaced on the centre of the table. The wine waiter took his place and Clifford chose a Chardonnay. Whilst the wine was being uncorked, sampled and poured, Clarice pretended to scan the menu, her heart pounding in her chest. *I really must learn to read!* she thought.

'Chin chin,' Clifford said, raising his wine glass.

Clarice clinked her glass to his and took a tiny sip. She had not eaten all day in order to save her pennies, and it wouldn't do to get tipsy.

'Now what shall we have to eat?' Clifford mused, his nose buried in his menu.

'I really can't decide,' Clarice said, snapping the card closed and placing it on the table. The only one who had noticed she'd been looking at it upside down was the wine waiter, and he'd wandered off with a smirk on his face.

'Neither can I, but I rather fancy the salmon.'

Clarice hated fish and her pulse raced. Clifford was not being helpful at all and now she wondered how to solve this latest conundrum.

'Then again...' Clifford began and Clarice's hopes rose. 'The steak looks inviting.'

Thank God! 'Yes, I thought so too,' Clarice said.

'Jolly good.' Clifford caught the waiter's eye and beckoned him over. 'The lady will have the steak, please, and so will I.'

'How would you like it cooked, madam?' the waiter asked.

Clarice had picked up her glass and another small sip afforded her time to think. 'Well done, please.'

The waiter wrinkled his nose very slightly and, turning to Clifford, asked, 'And for sir?'

'Medium rare.'

'Very good, sir.' With that, the waiter rushed off to place the order with the chef.

'Now, m'dear, tell me about your day,' Clifford said, focusing all his attention on his dinner date.

Oh, Lord, more lies! Clarice thought as she began. 'Like I said, my allowance cheque is late again so I wrote to Daddy.'

Clifford nodded. 'Where is your father?'

'Oh, he's in America, New York to be precise. He's out there negotiating a deal on a hotel.'

'Buying or selling?' Clifford asked.

'Buying, of course,' Clarice answered with a little giggle. 'How was your day?' The change of subject was somewhat abrupt, but she had to turn the conversation around to him before she found herself so deep in fantasy she could lose her way.

'I had lunch with my pater,' Clifford informed her.

Clarice had no idea what a pater was so she just nodded.

'Yes, he wants me to go into the family business, but I'm undecided as yet.'

Well, that answered that question; his pater was his father. 'So what is this business?'

'Construction. Father travels the country as well as abroad building houses, pubs and hotels. Anywhere there's spare land, he'll build on it, subject to contract, of course.'

Just then their food was delivered and Clarice's mouth watered at the aroma from the juicy steak, roast potatoes and vegetables. Now knowing which of the cutlery to use, Clarice smiled widely at her paramour.

Little more was said as they both tucked into their food hungrily. When the meal was finished and paid for, Clifford retrieved their coats, helping Clarice into hers first. Outside he hailed a cab and Clarice felt her blood run cold. Where were they off to now and could she be dead by the morning?

12

Jared was in the yard, overseeing the return of the tatters, when a very excited Seth jumped from his cart and ran across to his friend.

'Jared, I've met a girl!' he said breathlessly.

'Please don't tell me her name is Clarice,' Jared replied with a forced grin.

'No, her name is Judith Kingston and she has blonde hair and the brightest blue eyes!' Seth responded dreamily.

The others ambled over to see what all the fuss was about.

'Oh, blimey, that's all we'll hear about from now on,' Johnny put in with a laugh when Seth repeated his description of the pretty girl. At nineteen years old, Johnny was the youngest of the group and always had something to say about everything, regardless of whether it concerned him or not.

'Belt up,' Dan said, giving Johnny a playful push, which made his titian hair fall over his eyes.

'Well, I'm pleased for you, Seth,' Sam said, feeling a little jealous.

'Thanks, mate,' Seth replied.

'You can tell us all about her on the walk home, but first let's get these horses seen to, please.' Jared waved a hand as if in gentle dismissal.

Seth received pats on the back as the lads dispersed to feed the equine family.

Eventually home time came and Seth began his tale as the tatters gathered. 'She came to my cart and told me her name was Judith.'

'What, before you asked?' Paul enquired.

'Nooo, I asked first,' Seth said.

'Where does she live?' This came from Tom who was at the back of the group.

Seth peered over his shoulder to answer. 'The Unicorn in Smithfield Street.'

Jared thought for a moment then asked, 'What the hell were you doing over there? Your round was nowhere near Smithfield Street.'

'I know but I was doing no good business at all so I made a detour – and I'm bloody glad I did!'

Jared shook his head and sighed. He couldn't really say much to that as he'd done the same thing when he was on the road and McGuire hadn't taken him to task over it.

'Any road up,' Seth went on, 'I'm going to see her dad tonight and ask his permission for Judith to walk out with me.'

'Crikey, Seth, you don't let the grass grow under your feet!' Sam exclaimed.

'No point, is there? Look what happened to McGuire, he had to wait a lifetime to wed Alice.'

Everyone nodded at the truth of Seth's statement.

'We'd best hurry up then because you're going to need a bath,' Jared said.

Seth's horror-stricken countenance made them all fall about

laughing. A bath once a month was sufficient and it hadn't come to that time yet.

'Are you nervous, about asking Judith's dad, I mean?' Dan asked as they trudged homeward.

'To be honest – I'm shit-scared!'

Again, laughter sounded loudly, causing people passing by to glance in their direction with frowns. Clearly they thought the boys were rabble-rousers.

'Would you like some company?' Jared asked.

'Yeah, I would,' Seth replied gratefully.

'There you go, lads, a night in the pub it is then,' Johnny said, rubbing his hands together.

'As long as you don't drink so much that you can't turn in for work tomorrow,' Jared warned.

Parting ways, they hurried home to eat, wash and change their clothes before all meeting up again later outside the Unicorn.

Once home, Jared re-kindled the range and placed a large meat pie inside to heat through while Seth peeled potatoes and set them to boil. Covered in gravy and with a few vegetables, it would provide a hearty meal and put a lining on their stomachs.

Whilst the food was cooking, they each had a good strip wash and shave then laid out their decent clothes on their beds.

Seth was pathering in the kitchen in just his underclothes, willing the spuds to cook quicker.

'We have loads of time yet, Seth; why don't you make a cuppa?'

'Yes, tea. I'll make a drink. Cups, milk – oh, hell, I'm a mess, Jared!'

With a grin, Jared made his friend sit at the table. 'You stay there, I'll do it.'

A little while later, the pals were enjoying a steaming

beverage and a hot meal. Even as he chewed the last morsel, Seth was out of his chair and running upstairs to get dressed.

Jared shook his head with a smile. He knew how his friend was feeling because hadn't he felt the same when he visited Clarice Connaught? Jared had experienced the butterflies in his belly. Poor Seth, he would be like a cat on a hot tin roof until he'd spoken to Mr Kingston. Jared sent up a prayer that the man would give Seth his blessing because if he refused there would be no consoling his housemate.

The other friends were gathered outside the public house when Jared and Seth arrived, then they all piled indoors. The bar was full of men dressed in working clothes and so deep in conversation that no one noticed the coterie as they pushed forward to the counter. Gas lights lit the room with a sickly yellow glow, highlighting a few tables and chairs and sending shadows into the corners. Fresh sawdust was strewn on the floor to absorb any spillages and cigarette smoke pervaded the air in grey spirals. Despite its poor appearance, it seemed like a jolly place, laughter and banter resounding here and there.

Jared tapped a coin on the long counter and a pretty young blonde girl responded immediately. So this must be Judith, he thought.

'Seven pints of porter, please.'

'Coming right up,' she said jovially.

Judith smiled and began the task of pouring the beer. Her gaze settled on Seth and she beamed with delight at seeing him again. For his part, Seth blushed to the roots of his hair whilst his pals nudged him, big grins on their faces.

As each glass was poured, it was passed back to one of the others and once the last one was ready, Jared paid. After depositing the money in the till, Judith approached and spoke to the man working by her side. She pointed to Seth and the man whom Jared assumed was her father nodded. Mr Kingston was a kindly looking fellow, but built like a bear and it was clear to all that he would brook no nonsense in his alehouse. He crooked a finger to Seth, beckoning him.

'Oh, God!' Seth whispered as he passed his beer to Jared to hold.

'Go to it, Seth,' Jared replied. He watched as Mr Kingston lifted the end of the counter and led Seth through to a back room. 'Fingers crossed, boys, for Daniel has entered the den of the lion.'

The next ten minutes were pure torment for them as they awaited the return of their friend. Would it be smiles and happiness for Seth or would it be tears and misery?

13

Whilst the tatters were praying Seth would win Mr Kingston around, Clarice was sitting in the carriage feeling decidedly uncomfortable. More than that, she was afraid. She had no idea where Clifford was taking her, and she began to wonder if she should feign illness and ask to be taken home. Just as she was about to speak, the carriage jolted to a halt.

Clifford climbed out and extended a hand for Clarice to do the same. Once the cabbie was paid, the two entered a massive building. Dark and dingy on the outside, the interior was well lit and full of people. Clarice breathed a sigh of relief as she was guided into a huge room full of gaming tables. Clifford had brought her to a gambling den!

Shouting and applause drew her eyes to a blackjack table where a fellow was being congratulated on his win.

With coats checked in, Clifford greeted folk he was clearly well acquainted with, introducing 'Clara' as they threaded their way through the crowd. Clifford saw the looks of envy on the faces of the men he spoke to at being out with such a beautiful woman and he revelled in it. Clarice, for her part, smiled sweetly as she shook hands with one after another of Clifford's acquaintances then raised her eyes adoringly to Clifford.

'So, m'dear, what do you fancy?' Clifford asked. 'Poker, blackjack, baccarat, roulette – it's all here and it is most certainly time to have some fun.'

'You go ahead, Clifford, I'm afraid I'm in no position to gamble until my allowance comes through,' Clarice said quietly, again reinforcing the idea that she needed money.

'Don't you worry about that,' he said, pulling out his wallet and handing over a bundle of notes to the cashier who exchanged them for chips. Passing them to Clarice, he added, 'You go and enjoy yourself.'

Clarice smiled as she took the box of chips and, reaching up onto her tiptoes, she whispered in his ear, 'Thank you.' Then a little louder added, 'I think I'll try poker, although I've never played before.' The lie slipped easily from her tongue. She had grown up playing the game with her father, along with many other card games, and she was really rather good at it.

They wandered over to the card table and a space was made for her by a gentleman who threw down his cards in despair before heading to the bar.

'Clifford darling, you'll have to help me because I have no idea what to do.' Clarice raised her voice a tad so the other players could hear her over the noise of the room. A quick glance around the table showed her ruse had worked for the gamers smiled at the prospect of taking her chips.

The first hand was dealt and Clarice chirped, 'Oh, aren't the cards pretty?' Giving the impression she was just a dizzy-brained female all added to her persona and when she asked, 'What do I do now?' her fellow gamers could barely contain their smirks.

Clifford guided her through the first hand and Clarice deliberately lost her bet, a pout and groan solidifying the mens' notions that they would fleece her in no time. Clifford stroked her cheek, saying, 'Bad luck, dearest.'

The next game began and Clifford leaned over her shoulder.

'May I play this hand myself, do you think?' Clarice asked, much to the glee of the others around her.

'Of course, but watch this lot for they are all thieves,' Clifford answered with a laugh.

Clarice watched carefully and as the game progressed she made her bet. By the end, she won the pot, much to the chagrin of the other players. 'Oh, look, I won!' Clarice said, clapping her hands daintily.

'Well done, Clara!' Clifford praised.

The evening wore on and Clarice ensured she didn't win each time but by the end of the night she had amassed quite a hefty sum. She collected her winnings, saying it was time to go home. She politely thanked her adversaries for teaching her how to play and she and Clifford went to exchange the chips back into cash. Going to get their coats, Clifford said, 'My, but you were lucky this evening.'

He helped her into her coat as she answered, 'Wasn't I? Of course, the money belongs to you as you gave it to me in the first place.'

'Nonsense, m'dear, those are your winnings, enjoy them.'

Clarice smiled up adoringly at Clifford, saying, 'You're so good to me.'

Clifford's chest puffed up and he tipped the hat girl as she passed him his coat and top hat.

'Clifford, please say we can come here again, I so enjoyed myself tonight.'

'Your wish is my command, dear,' he responded.

In no time, Clarice had begun to ensure the two might

become an item and she intended to hold onto him – at least until he was of no further use to her.

Chatting excitedly in the cab back to the hotel, Clarice showered her beau with praise and compliments. It was down to him, she said, that she'd had such a good time; she couldn't possibly have won without his guiding hand.

Clifford drank it all in, loving the fact that Clara Christian doted on him. He was falling in love and there was nothing he could do to stop himself. Despite being twice her age, Clifford knew how he felt about her and clearly she felt the same, otherwise she would have told him to take a running jump. He found himself wondering what she saw in him but also thinking he would do anything for this young woman.

Clarice, however, had different ideas. As Clara, she would simper all she could to extract as much as possible from the gullible Clifford. As Clarice, though, she would hold on to her new-found independence, and woe betide anyone who tried to take it from her.

Now she had enough money to stay at the boarding house for a month if she wanted to as well as buy herself a new winter coat.

And now she knew where the casino was, she could go back anytime to boost her coffers. She wondered if she'd be allowed in on her own, as lone women didn't usually socialise unaccompanied. There was only one way to find out and that was to visit again, this time without Clifford breathing down her neck.

At the Midland Hotel, Clifford drew Clarice into his arms and after a slight pause he kissed her goodnight on her cheek. He desperately wanted to kiss her lips but was afraid of frightening her away by being too forward. Although he had only known her for such a short while, Clifford was so in love he couldn't bear the thought of losing her. After arranging to collect her at seven o'clock the following evening, Clifford watched her walk the few steps away from him and his heart felt the sting of longing. He didn't want to let her go even for a moment.

As was now becoming customary, Clarice stepped into the hotel until Clifford had gone then once more slipped out and hurried back to the boarding house.

Once in her room, she spread out her winnings on the bed. Her smile turned to laughter as she counted up ten pounds.

'Thank you very much, gentlemen,' she whispered as she gathered the notes and rolled them into a bundle. She would put it down her chemise for safe keeping until she could open a bank account. Clarice Connaught intended to discover the whereabouts of other casinos where she could spend her days parting men from their money.

That night, Clarice dreamt she was a millionairess – her riches made from her life as a gambler.

14

When Seth walked back into the bar, his face was as white as a sheet and his eyes were glazed over. It was as if he was moving in a trance.

The boys exchanged a glance and Sam, to prevent his laughter exploding, sucked in his lips and clamped them together with his teeth. Tom removed his cap and scratched his scalp before replacing it in a more comfortable position. Dan rocked back on his heels and inspected his shiny toecaps. Paul suddenly found something very interesting to look at on the ceiling and Jared closed his eyes tight for a moment then took a drink of his ale. Johnny, in his inimitable way, pushed his head forward and said, 'Well?'

Seth stared at him for a long moment then took his glass of beer from Jared and downed it in one. Only then did he answer. 'Mr Kingston... he said... yes!'

Laughter and cheers erupted as they all clinked glasses and patted Seth on the back.

Behind the bar, Judith embraced her father before they once more began to serve thirsty customers.

'Next one is on me,' Seth said and another cheer rang out.

With fresh drinks in their hands, the conversation turned to where Seth would take Judith on their first date.

'I thought the music hall,' Seth said.

'Good choice, it's always a good night out,' Jared concurred.

'The weather's on the turn, so Park Street Gardens might be nice before it gets too cold,' Sam added, pleased when Seth nodded.

'The winter could be a problem, though,' Seth muttered.

'Well, you'll have to come in here to see her, just don't get too plastered while you watch her working!' Johnny said with a laugh.

'Will her dad give her time off?' Jared asked.

'I bloody hope so now I've gone through all this!'

Again, the boys' laughter rang out.

'You'd best start saving your pennies,' Paul put in.

'What for?' Seth asked.

'She'll most likely want a big wedding,' Paul responded with a grin.

'Oh, Christ!' Seth mumbled into his glass.

The boys chatted quietly over their pints and for a while Jared watched the older men in the bar playing dominoes, an occasional knock on the table saying a player had to miss a turn. Friendly banter was taking place as the black and white counters were slapped down forming a snake-like pattern on the tabletop. In another corner, a game of tabletop skittles was being played out with shouts of delight as the pins fell noisily. Elsewhere shove ha'penny caused raucous laughter as a man swore loudly when his coin failed to land in the bed he'd aimed for.

'What do you think?' Seth asked Jared quietly.

'About what?'

'Judith!' Seth replied.

'She's very pretty. Seems friendly too. I think you're onto a winner there, mate,' Jared said.

'So do I.'

'Just don't bugger it up!' Johnny put in.

Dan just blew out his cheeks, exasperated with Johnny yet again pushing into the others' conversation.

'He won't,' Sam added.

'Right, I'm for home,' Jared said, placing his empty glass on the bar. The others agreed and while they finished their ale, Seth went to say goodnight to Judith and her father.

The men in the bar shouted, 'Tarrar, lads,' as the boys gave a wave and left the pub.

Walking back, they continued to tease Seth about taking care with Judith lest her father seek him out with a shotgun. Seth took it all good-naturedly and eventually they veered off back to their respective homes.

Back at the house, Jared made up their snap tins for the following day whilst Seth made tea and a sandwich which they consumed in the kitchen.

'Thanks for tonight, Jared, I appreciate you all being there for me.'

'I have to say you had us worried there for a minute. You looked like you'd seen a ghost.'

'I couldn't believe it when Mr Kingston agreed to me walking out with Judith, although he did lay down some rules; not to keep her out late and definitely no hanky-panky!'

Jared grinned. 'I know you'll treat her like a lady, mate. You'll have to take her to Dudley to meet your mum as well.'

'Mum's gonna love her, I just know it,' Seth said with a contented sigh.

'She's a nice girl, Seth, you're a lucky bloke,' Jared said in all honesty.

'Thanks, pal. Hey, you know what – you're my best man if it ever comes to it.'

'It would be my pleasure. I can tell everyone what a stinker you used to be when I first met you.'

'You wouldn't dare – would you?' Jared shook his head and Seth blurted out, 'You bugger!'

'What was it you said the other day? Eloquently put! Seriously, though, Seth, if you might be thinking about marriage in the future you should also consider where you would live because there's not much room here.'

'I suppose it would make sense to move into the pub, that way Judith can still work there if she wants to.'

'That would be sensible. Would you stay on the rounds or help out in the bar, do you think? Although I think we're getting ahead of ourselves here.' Jared winked.

'I'd prefer to keep tatting. Then I could look forward to going home to my wife. Besides, I wouldn't want to work with her dad; from what I know, sons-in-law can't put a foot right so...'

'I'd heard that too,' Jared said, stifling a yawn. 'Well, just see how it goes first, eh. You did well this evening to ask her dad. She's a lucky lass. Anyway, I'm going to my bed now, I'll see you in the morning.'

'G'night, mate.' Seth watched his friend scratching his buttock as he disappeared through the door leading to the stairs. Seth lingered a while longer, watching the dying embers in the range. He considered himself a very fortunate young man to have such good mates and now a lovely girl to call his own. Maybe one day they *would* wed and have a family. The thought brought a smile to his lips and again he conjured an image of Judith in his mind.

Snapping himself out of his reverie, he closed the range doors, ensured the doors and windows were secure and, dousing the lamps, he too went to his bed.

15

Clarice had been gone for a few days now and John Connaught knew in his heart she wasn't likely to return. He had tried his best to raise her after his wife had died but Clarice was head-strong and wilful. They had both mourned the loss of Jenny in their own way, he was quiet and sombre, while Clarice ran riot and caused havoc.

Sitting before the fire, his mind took him back in time to when he had been summoned to the school. The headmistress had told him in no uncertain terms that Clarice could not continue to attend. She was stealing from the other children, fighting and refusing to do her work, leaving her unable to read or write. John had taken her home and she had never set foot on any school premises again.

John sighed loudly then sipped his cocoa. He had tried to teach her himself by playing card games but suspected she only memorised the suits, pictures and numbers. Regardless, she was a quick learner and won almost every game. This was what puzzled him, why she could pick things up so easily but never applied herself. Clarice could have made something of her life, she could have found a good job and earned a decent wage. Instead, she lounged around the house, only occasionally cooking a meal or washing their clothes.

Clarice had taught herself to cook and was very good at it but she had no interest in it. All she ever seemed to do with her time was spread malicious gossip about her father. It was like a game to her, and the more the neighbours believed her, the better she liked it.

The only sounds in the room now were the ticking of the old tin clock on the mantelpiece and the crackling of the fire. John realised he missed having his daughter around the place, although he was glad there was no more arguing. For years they had yelled at each other, never able to agree upon anything. Clarice, when in one of her moods, could pick a fight with her own fingernails. How was it she had turned out this way? Both he and Jenny were mild of manner but Clarice was like a wildcat.

John had considered searching harder to find his daughter but was certain that even if he did, she wouldn't come home. She would more than likely make a scene and have him hauled away by the constabulary. So he had decided not to bother, Clarice had made her choice. He just prayed that wherever she was, she was safe. After all, if she ever turned up on his doorstep, he would take her in, no questions asked. She was his daughter, for better or worse.

* * *

Clarice was donning the best clothes she owned and was ready to set out on another adventure. She was going back to the casino where she hoped they would not turn her away because she was unaccompanied. She needed to win more money as her ten pounds wouldn't last long if she were to buy new clothes, but she also wanted to discover the whereabouts of other casinos. It would not do to keep winning in the same establishment and arouse suspicion upon herself. She was an excellent card player but proving she was not cheating could be difficult. Therefore, she intended to use her talents at as many places as possible.

Hailing a cab, she climbed aboard, her nerves jangling. She prayed it would all go well because if not she would have to explain herself to Clifford the next time they went together. They were sure to visit the place again and undoubtedly someone would tell him about her trying to get in.

As the cab rolled over the cobblestones, Clarice patted her dark hair which was coiled neatly beneath her small teardrop hat. She breathed deeply, willing her anxiety to melt away. With legs crossed, her right foot beat a tattoo into empty space and her fingers kept time on the bag on her lap.

Arriving at her destination, she paid the cabbie and walked to the door of the property. To all intents and purposes, the building looked very much like all the others in the street; covered in grime and not really worth a second glance.

Clarice suddenly thought, what if it's not open during the daytime?

Knowing there was only one way to find out, she swallowed hard and rapped the knocker. A moment later, the door opened and she was faced with a giant of a man.

'Miss Christian. How nice to see you again, so soon too.' A wide smile split the face of the man as he stood aside to enable her to enter.

'Thank you... erm?'

'Silas,' he answered as she lifted her skirt and daintily stepped inside. His eyes swept over her approvingly before he closed the door. 'May I escort you?'

'That would be most welcome, Silas, thank you.'

Once they had checked in her coat at the cloakroom, and after exchanging her money for chips, together they walked towards the brightly lit card room and headed for the table she had sat at the previous evening. Taking a seat, Clarice inclined her head in thanks and Silas wandered away.

Casting a glance around, Clarice was surprised at how busy it was at this time of the day. She was greeted politely by the other gamers at the table as she piled her counters on the green baize.

Nodding to the dealer, Clarice was ready to part these fine gentlemen from their cash. Again she determined she would not win every game even if it looked like she might; she didn't want to find herself banned. Besides, it could be there were better players than herself around the table today.

Play began in earnest and Clarice was surprised at how she was treated with the utmost respect. One gent bought her a drink and another moved away politely to smoke his cigar so the smoke wouldn't make her cough.

Each time Clarice won, she was congratulated amid the laughter and the odd grumble from one of the losers. The atmosphere around the table was jovial and the noise attracted others to watch the games taking place.

Eventually Clarice thought it was time to quit and return to the boarding house so she could get ready for her evening out with Clifford. Once she had cashed in her chips, she gave Silas a large tip and he opened the door and hailed her a cab.

During the time she had spent at the gaming table, Clarice had not only won a hefty pot, but she had also learned of other places she could go to supplement her earnings.

In the cab home, she congratulated herself. Happy she could pay her bill as well as ensure a roof over her head for a while to come without a worry, Clarice smiled inwardly. Not only that but she could afford to buy herself a couple of new dresses. She had planned to do this from her previous winnings and now she knew she could purchase some good quality garments which would last. Smiling to herself, Clarice patted her bag which held her winnings. She was most definitely on her way up the social ladder now and nothing was going to stop her reaching the top.

16

It had rained heavily during the night and the petrichor was strong in Jared's nose as he and Seth trudged across the heath to the yard. There was a definite chill in the air which seemed to seep through his jacket in search of his bones. Before very long, he would have to don his overcoat, for winter was on her way, eagerly pushing aside the beautiful autumn.

Reaching the yard, he beckoned the Cavenor brothers, saying, 'I think we'll light the braziers today, so leave the big gates open but come inside and shut the doors.'

'Thanks, Boss,' Dicky said, grateful not to have to stand guard in the cold.

'Mr Bobby, give the old range a clear out of ashes and set it going if you wouldn't mind, then we can all have a hot drink. I've brought some fresh milk and there should be tea and sugar on the shelf.'

'Will do, Boss.'

Jared settled himself in the office, listening to his workforce arriving and grumbling about the change in the weather. His thoughts turned to Clarice Connaught and where she might be now. He hoped she was somewhere safe and warm; it would do a body no good to be out on the street at this time of year.

Three large braziers soon had the workshop cosy and warm and the small range chased the chill from the office.

An hour after he had arrived, there was a knock on the open door and one of the grooms said, 'Sorry to bother you, Boss, but Sam ain't come in as yet. I thought you should know.'

'Thanks, Joe,' Jared replied, 'maybe his bed was too comfortable to leave this morning.' The two shared a chuckle but as the groom returned to the stables, Jared's smile turned to a frown. It was not like Sam to be late, in fact he was usually one of the first in.

Jared decided to give it an hour or so and if Sam wasn't anywhere to be seen then maybe he would call round to the house.

By ten o'clock, Sam still hadn't put in an appearance, so Jared left the office and strode across to the stable. 'Can you hitch Bess to the cart, please? I'm going to Sam's house. Something must be wrong for him to miss work.'

The stable hands quickly did his bidding and in ten minutes Jared was on the road. Travelling up Adderley Street, the cart passed a school where children ran around shouting and laughing during their long-awaited playtime. Normally Jared would have smiled at their antics but today he was too worried about Sam to take much notice. Opposite was a public house from which came the sound of a piano being played with gusto. Passing the milk cart where the milkman banged on an empty churn and called out his wares, Bess moved on. Jared gently tugged on the rein to steer Bess beneath the viaduct before turning into Bromley Street. Pulling Bess to a halt, Jared jumped down and rapped the knocker on Sam's front door. A moment later, it was opened by his friend, whose red and puffy eyes made it plain to see that he had been crying.

'Jared, come in. I'm sorry but...' Sam closed the door as Jared stepped inside.

'What's happened?' Jared asked but he'd already guessed as he'd noticed all the curtains were still closed.

'My mum died last night,' Sam said quietly as he led Jared into the kitchen.

'Oh, mate, I'm so sorry.' Jared took the chair offered and accepted the tea poured for him.

'I'm waiting for the undertaker. The doctor has already been,' Sam said as he too took a chair.

'How did she...?' Jared began.

'Natural causes, the doctor said. She was old, I suppose, although I didn't think so.'

Jared's mind took him back eight years to when his own mum had died from starvation; feeding her children rather than herself. Then, just hours later, his younger sister passed from the illness ravaging her little body. The pain of their loss stabbed again and his heart went out to his friend.

'I know it might not be the time to ask but can you afford the funeral because if not...'

'Thanks, but it's all paid up. I just have to arrange a date with the funeral director.'

'Well, that's one thing less for you to worry about. If there's anything I can do to help, you only have to ask.'

'There is one thing – would you and the lads come to the funeral?'

'Of course. In fact, I'll shut the yard for the day.'

'I'll need to arrange a wake as well,' Sam said.

'Any of the pubs would be happy to sort that out for you.

They can put on a decent spread but I don't know how much they would charge,' Jared offered.

'I'll have enough to cover it from my savings,' Sam replied.

Jared nodded. 'Have you got a suit?'

'Yes.'

'Sam, what about the house?'

'It belongs to me now. My dad worked at the bank and he bought it just before he died, luckily for Mum and me.'

Just then, there was a knock on the door and Sam got to his feet. 'That'll be the undertaker.'

As Sam went to answer the door, Jared blew out his cheeks. He really had hoped Sam had only overslept this morning; he had never expected to walk into a house full of sadness. He waited patiently while Sam oversaw the sad business of his mum being taken away with all the respect and reverence afforded by the undertaker and his staff. Hearing the front door close, Jared steeled himself for Sam's return to the kitchen. He knew from experience that his friend would feel lost and alone, and that tears and heartache would come and go in vast waves. All Jared could do was to be there to listen while Sam talked and reminisced.

Sam entered the kitchen and stood looking at Jared. 'She's gone.'

Jared was instantly on his feet, wrapping his muscular arms about Sam, holding him gently while the young man's heart broke and his tears fell like rain. Jared's eyes pricked as he tried in vain to hold back his own emotions.

In the quiet darkness of the kitchen, the two friends cried, holding on to each other, cementing their bonds of friendship even tighter.

After a while, Sam's sobs receded and the young men let go of each other.

'Thanks, Jared. Shouldn't you be getting back to the yard?' Sam said with a sniff.

Shaking his head, Jared replied, 'There's no rush, they know where I am. Besides, being here with you is more important.'

The following few hours were spent with Sam talking and Jared listening. 'Mum could be overbearing at times. She treated me like I was five years old. *Don't forget to wash behind your ears. Eat all your vegetables, there's a good boy.* It was only when I started coming to your house to play cards that she began to realise I was growing up.'

Jared smiled. 'You were lucky to have her as long as you did, I wish I had been so fortunate. Take some time, Sam, as long as you need, before coming back to work. On the other hand, though, don't sit here moping. You know where I live if you feel the need to get out of the house.'

Jared left only after ensuring Sam would be as well as could be expected, saying, 'Let me know if you need anything.'

Travelling back to the yard, Jared decided he would share Sam's sad news when everyone returned that evening.

There was a shout which made him halt Bess and a woman in a tattered dress rushed over to him, a bundle of rags in her arms. 'How much, cocker?' With more gaps than teeth and hair in disarray, the woman threw the bundle up to him.

Feeling dreadfully sorry for her, Jared replied, 'Tuppence, Mother.'

'Ooh, ta!' the woman replied, rubbing her bony hands together.

Tossing the rags into the cart, Jared dug in his pocket for some coins. 'I don't have any change so you'll have to have a threepenny bit.'

The woman danced a little jig then caught the twelve-sided coin and gave it a kiss. 'Ta very much, lad.'

Jared smiled and clucked to Bess. He hadn't thought to bring a satchel of pennies with him when he'd set out, he just needed to get to Sam's.

Pulling in through the open gates, Jared let out a shrill whistle and the large door opened for him to enter. A stable lad came running and Jared thanked the boy who unhitched Bess and took her to the stable.

'All right, Boss?' Dicky asked.

Jared nodded then said quietly, 'Sam's mum has passed away. I'll call a meeting later to let everyone else know.'

'That's a shame,' Bobby said.

'Yeah, Sam's a mess so he won't be in for a few days.'

Jared left the brothers warming their hands on the brazier and climbing the steps he entered the office. Sitting in the big chair, he leaned back and allowed his thoughts to roam. Death was always lurking around the corner and could come for anyone at any time. With a shudder, he buried his head in a ledger.

17

Clarice was ready and waiting outside the Midland Hotel when Clifford arrived by cab. If her luck at the tables held, she would be able to book a room here and end the charade.

'My sweet, I've thought of nothing but you all day!' Clifford gushed.

'And I, of you.' The lie slipped easily from Clarice's tongue as she stepped into the carriage.

'Dinner first, then the theatre perhaps?'

Clarice didn't hide her disappointment and pouted like a small child.

'Is something wrong, my love?' Clifford asked, full of concern at her silence.

'No, it's just that...'

Clifford waited then urged, 'Go on, m'dear.'

'Well, it was so very exciting at the casino last evening, I was wondering...' Clarice paused.

Clifford took up the idea quickly as was her plan. 'Of course, if you'd like to go back, then we shall.'

'Are there any other places we might visit, darling?' Clarice fawned.

'Why, yes. We shall find you another casino where you can try your beginner's luck again.'

'Thank you, Clifford, you are so good to me.'

'Clara, I adore you and would do anything for you, surely you know that by now?'

Clarice inclined her head shyly and, lifting her gloved hand to her mouth, she kissed her fingers then laid them on his cheek.

Clifford placed his hand over hers then suddenly the cab jolted to a stop, throwing them closer together.

Still playing the coy maiden, Clarice quickly pulled away from him before he had the idea that he should kiss her. She didn't particularly want to be kissed by this man, she only wanted him for what he could give her in exchange for as little as possible on her part.

They entered the restaurant and were shown to a table lit by a single candle. A waiter brought them menus and again Clarice's pulse raced. She really would have to learn to read properly.

'What takes your fancy, m'dear?' Clifford asked without taking his eyes from his menu card.

Clarice gave an audible sigh which brought Clifford's eyes to hers in question. 'I don't know what I'm in the mood for,' she said.

'I think I'll have the veal,' he said, handing the card to the waiter.

Clarice made the pretence of studying the writing further then said, 'Yes, me too.'

The waiter scurried away to the kitchen with their orders and wine was poured.

'It's lovely here,' Clarice said, glancing around. *And dark*, she thought, glad she would not be recognised in the dim lighting. Then again, no one she knew would frequent a place such as this. Those people would be more at home in a spit and sawdust pub.

'You are lovely,' Clifford responded dreamily.

Clarice smiled then went on. 'So tell me where we're going later.' She gave a little shrug, a childish gesture of excitement.

'Much the same, sweetheart, and hopefully you will have Lady Luck on your side again.'

It certainly wouldn't hurt, Clarice thought as she clinked her wine glass to his.

After they had eaten, they were on the move, then welcomed warmly into another gambling house.

Making straight for the card table playing blackjack, Clarice asked to be allowed to join their company. A seat was drawn up for her and Clifford stood behind her. A waitress arrived to exchange the few pounds she had brought with her for chips, which Clarice laid on the green baize and her nod told the dealer she was ready.

The cards were dealt and Clarice lifted the corner of hers then glanced up at Clifford and at his smile she made her bet. At another nod, Clarice received her second card which again she peeped at. Giving a little sigh, Clarice again looked to Clifford for his advice. He squeezed her shoulder gently and she increased her bet then knocked on the table, telling the dealer she was sticking.

The others around the table watched with interest, and when Clarice turned her hand over, they applauded her win. The dealer paid up with a smile, inclining his head in a congratulatory manner. Clarice played the next few rounds almost flippantly, both winning and losing against her fellow players, but by the end of the night she was well in pocket.

Clifford retrieved her coat after she had cashed in her chips, saying, 'You really are the luckiest person I've ever met.'

Skill, not luck, Clarice thought but instead she just smiled sweetly. 'I do love our evenings at these places and I couldn't do it without your help.'

'Then we shall come again; anything to please you, my darling,' Clifford said as the cab rolled its way back to the Midland Hotel.

Whilst Clarice had been enjoying herself in the gambling house, Seth had gone to have tea with the Kingstons, leaving Jared alone in the house. After his evening meal, Jared walked over to Bromley Street to spend some time with Sam. He knew what it was like to be on your own whilst in mourning and he didn't want his friend to suffer the same fate.

After being invited in, Jared was relieved that Sam was pleased to see him. Over tea, Sam explained that his mum's funeral was to take place the following week.

'That's quick,' Jared remarked.

'The weather's on the turn so they want to get as many funerals as possible over and done with before the ground is too hard to dig.'

'Bloody hell, did they say that?' Jared asked with surprise.

'No, they didn't come right out with it, but I'm guessing that's the reason,' Sam said. 'The service is at two o'clock on Friday next at St Bartholomew's.'

'We'll all be there,' Jared assured him.

'I'm dreading it.'

'I can understand that, but at least you can say a final goodbye and see her off in style. I wish I could have done the same for my sister and mum.'

'I'm sorry, Jared, but you must be happy to know they're in heaven now.'

Jared gave a nod. He'd never been much of a worshipper and losing his family in the way he had compounded his disbelief in a God who would allow it to happen. He kept his thoughts to himself, however, and was glad when the conversation turned to more pleasant things. He again related the tale of Seth and Judith and how smitten the young man was.

'Have you thought any more about trying to find Clarice?' Sam asked suddenly.

'No – well – what would be the point? She could be anywhere by now.'

'I suppose so, it's a shame, though.'

'Clearly it wasn't meant to be,' Jared said with a shrug but deep in his heart the ache was still there. He knew the only way to conquer it would be to meet someone else, but with his job it was most unlikely. Maybe it was time he and the lads went out more in the evenings; the music hall, maybe. He would suggest it but not until Mrs Jenkins's funeral had taken place, then perhaps Sam would be more inclined to join them.

'Seth's a lucky bloke to have met Judith,' Sam said. 'I think I need a wife.'

'Me an' all,' Jared concurred.

As if reading his thoughts, Sam added, 'We should go out and find one.'

Jared grinned as they clinked teacups.

'To getting married.'

'To wedded bliss for us all,' Sam said.

18

The following morning, Jared called a meeting and explained to all about Sam's mother having passed away and what time and where the funeral would be held. Then he suggested they all join him at the pub for a drink that night. He said he would see if Sam would come along too so they could show their support for the lad in his hour of need. Naturally everyone agreed, even the Cavenor brothers said they would be there. So the time was set for eight o'clock at the Unicorn on Smithfield Street, the Kingstons' pub, where Seth could meet with Judith again.

Going about their business, each of them carried a sadness at the news of Mrs Jenkins's death, despite only having met her a few times. Sam was one of their own and his unhappiness weighed heavily upon their shoulders.

As his friends and colleagues worked, Jared took out the map and began to plan a change in routes for the following week, but he found it hard to concentrate. His mind swung like a pendulum from poor Sam to where Clarice might be living now. For all he had only met her a couple of times, he could not get her out of his head. He was concerned for her welfare, of course, but he had to admit that it was his heart that hammered when he thought of her and he wondered if he would ever get over her. Could he have these feelings for anyone else, or would the memory of Clarice Connaught scupper his chances of finding a wife?

Pulling himself together, Jared studied the map laid out on the desk before him. He *had* to forget Clarice and get on with his life. Moreover, he had Sam to worry about. He and the others would not let their friend mourn alone, they would be by his side every step of the way. Solidarity was the key to overcoming adversity, and they would hold Sam safely in their loving embrace.

Leaving the map where it was, Jared left the office, descended the steps and walked to where the Cavenors were keeping warm by the braziers.

'All right, Boss?' Bobby asked.

Jared nodded as he stretched out his hands to the glowing coals. 'I'm looking forward to having a drink tonight.'

The brothers returned his nod, rubbing their hands together to keep the blood flowing and the cold at bay.

'Anyone know what's on at the Gaiety Palace?' Jared asked.

'The usual singers and comedians, I think,' Dicky answered.

'We could go and check it out after a couple of beers, it might cheer Sam up a bit,' Jared said thoughtfully.

'Yeah, good idea,' Bobby replied.

'Would you two be good enough to pop round to Bromley Street and tell Sam what we have planned? Be sure to persuade him to come along because it will do him good to get out of the house.'

'Righto,' the brothers said in unison and turned away from the brazier with reluctance.

Jared watched the sorters working steadily, their efforts keeping them warm.

'How are you doing, son?' Tim Johnson's voice was gentle in Jared's ear.

'I'm okay, Dad. It's cold today and I'm wondering what the weather has in store for us these next months.'

'What else is on your mind, lad?' Tim asked.

'I'm worried about Sam. I know how he's feeling,' Jared confessed.

'Ar, me too. I hope you're not still brooding over that girl.'

Jared gave a tight-lipped smile, knowing his father had seen through his façade.

'She's gone, Jared, to God knows where. You have to get over it.'

'I know, Dad, but it's hard. It's the not knowing where she is that's plaguing me.'

'I can see that. It would have been different if she'd told you to bugger off.' Jared grinned and nodded. 'Bide your time, son, there's someone out there for you. One day you'll look back on this and laugh.' Tim's words were accompanied by a pat on Jared's shoulder before Tim returned to resume sorting with the others.

I hope you're right, Jared thought as he watched his father walk to the pile of rags.

A while later, the Cavenors reported that Sam would meet them at the Unicorn at the appointed time.

'Thanks, fellas, get yourselves a cup of tea and warm up.'

With grateful nods, Bobby and Dicky left the office, glad to be allowed to stand by the braziers once more.

The rest of the day passed peacefully enough but the lads were cold to the bone when they drove their carts into the yard.

Jared watched them from the office doorway and thought the same as he did every year, *This really isn't a job for the winter.*

That evening, wrapped up against the plummeting temperature, the friends met outside the Unicorn and they were all pleased to see Sam. They each muttered their condolences to him on his sad loss before trundling indoors.

There was a huge fire burning in the grate which was belting out heat. An old lady sat in a captain's chair to the side of the fireplace, poker in hand. As self-designated keeper of the fire, she stoked it regularly in exchange for a tot or two of gin.

A large gasolier hung from the ceiling, casting a bright light over the punters sitting at tables or standing at the bar. The room could have done with a lick of whitewash but nobody seemed to care. Heavy curtains were drawn across the windows helping to retain the heat and sawdust was sprinkled fresh every day to soak up any spillages and vomit.

Seth and Judith greeted each other warmly as she served the beers, and her father gave the boys a welcoming wave.

'We're going to the Gaiety Palace later, can you come?' Seth called out to Judith over the noise in the bar. Looking to her father for permission, she grinned when he nodded. Judith had lost her mother when she was younger and despite her mourning had slipped easily into the role of helper to her father. She cleaned their private quarters, did their washing and cooked the odd meal, usually relying on whatever the pub cook provided. She was caring and considerate and had a sunny disposition. Judith Kingston was pretty, slim, had a good sense of humour and despite the many offers of courtship, she only had eyes for Seth.

'I'll get Pokey to stand in. He'll do it for a jug of ale for his old mother,' Joe answered.

Judith raced from the bar for a wash and change of clothes.

'Pokey?' asked Jared.

'Ar, Andy McNabb. They call him that on account of him always having his nose in other folks' business!'

Sam burst out laughing at the explanation and Jared's tension eased a little. He'd been concerned Sam might be too sad to enjoy the evening out.

An hour or so later, the jolly band of friends left the Unicorn and headed for the Palace.

As they lined up to pay, Jared noticed a couple at the head of the queue. He stared in disbelief and when Paul asked what was wrong, Jared pointed to the woman.

'Clarice,' was all he could manage to say.

Jared's friends also stared at the woman, then looked back at him.

'Keep my place, I'll be back in a minute,' Jared said as he stepped out of the line.

Sam followed close behind but said nothing. Approaching the couple at the front of the queue, Jared spoke quietly. 'Clarice?'

The woman turned and the colour drained from her face. Thinking quickly, she responded with, 'I'm sorry, I think you are mistaken.'

Instantly Jared suspected what she was about and, muttering an apology, he turned on his heel and, along with Sam, returned to his place.

Questioning looks met him but it was Sam who explained. 'It wasn't her.'

'It was.' Jared's voice was low and filled with sadness as he saw the puzzled expressions on his friends' faces. 'She's with a toff and pretended not to know me.'

'Why would she do that?' Dan asked.

'She's after climbing the social ladder, I reckon,' Johnny replied.

Jared nodded. 'That would be my guess.'

The queue shuffled forward a few steps and Judith patted Jared's arm. 'If she can do that to you, she's not worth it.'

The others agreed and Jared outwardly shook off the incident, but inside his heart cracked and he felt like crying. Clarice had treated him abominably but at least now he could see her for what she was. Clarice Connaught was a gold-digger and would probably never have been happy with a man like him anyway. Her father was right. She wanted money and prestige and was out to get it from someone like the gent who was fawning all over her.

'I'm sorry, pal,' Seth muttered, knowing how stuck Jared was on the girl.

Jared blew out his cheeks then said, 'It doesn't matter.'

Glances were exchanged and they all knew it most certainly did matter. Their mate had received a verbal slap in the face and they would stand by him while he tried to get over it.

Trying to lighten the mood, Judith said, 'My friend is singing here tonight, I'll see if she'll come and meet you all later.'

Their excitement bubbled over about possibly hobnobbing with a star of the stage and Jared tried his best to join in.

At last they entered and found their seats. The high ceiling held gasoliers which hung down to light the area. The stage was framed with heavy curtains both sides which were draped in deep scallops across the front. Seating was placed in a horseshoe shape around the orchestra pit and the boxes for the wealthier patrons sat on the walls as if glued in place. Balcony seats provided a good view of the whole room. The dark red and gold wallpaper was tired and peeling in places but no one seemed to notice or care.

People began to fill the auditorium and families with picnic baskets immediately started to eat whatever they had brought with them. Sandwiches and fruit, cake and bottles of water or ale for the adults were avidly consumed.

The audience settled down and the band struck up a merry tune after which a comedian strolled to the centre of the stage. 'I complained to my wife the other night about the vinegar having lumps in. She said that's because they were pickled onions!'

Laughter filled the auditorium before the man went on, 'The doctor said he'd put me on my feet again in two weeks. My pal asked, did he do it? I said yes, I had to sell my horse and trap to pay the bill!'

Laughs and a few loud groans rippled around the audience but Jared heard nothing. His mind was elsewhere as his eyes searched the boxes high up on the walls for signs of Clarice and her beau. Then he saw her, a smile plastered across her face. He watched her applaud along with everyone else as the comedian left the stage to be replaced by a singer. Jared dragged his eyes away from her as the band played their introduction, then the most gorgeous voice carried a song to the back of the music hall with seemingly no effort at all.

Suddenly Jared was mesmerised by the refrain sung so beautifully by the pretty girl standing all alone on the boards. Her blonde curls bounced in the gas light as she strolled around, her long dress hiding none of her curves. On the last note, the audience went wild, clapping and stamping their feet.

Jared found himself caught up in the fervour before silence fell and she began another song. Eventually the young woman curtsied and walked off stage as the compere reappeared. He was greeted with boos and cat-calls and bits of food were thrown at him. The poor man tried in vain to calm the audience but loud whistles drowned him out. In a panic, he called the singer out again and he rushed off as the audience's applause and cheers threatened to lift off the roof.

'They like my friend,' Judith yelled over the racket.

'It's no surprise, she has the voice of an angel,' Sam said loudly just as the noise died down.

Johnny dug him in the ribs, a grin splitting his face, and Sam blushed fiercely.

Song after song she sang, encouraging the audience to join in, and Jared realised he was quite enjoying himself. He glanced up at Clarice's box and saw it was empty. He had considered approaching Clarice again at the end of the entertainment, but she had scuppered that plan. Maybe it was for the best; it might have ended in an argument or even a fight with her *friend* if Jared pushed it too far.

It was happenstance that Jared had seen Clarice in the first place, and after the way she had rebuffed him, he finally began to believe he was better off without her. Each time he thought on it, it stung, but Judith was right – Clarice was not worth the worry.

Before he knew it, people started to leave the hall. Some were chatting and others were still singing.

'Hang on here, I'll pop round to see my friend, Rose. She'll want to meet you all, especially Seth,' Judith said with a smile as her sweetheart ran his hands over his hair.

A few moments later, Judith and her friend, arm in arm, walked towards the young men.

'Everyone, this is Rose Whitman,' Judith said, then one by one the friends introduced themselves.

'I'm very pleased to meet you all,' Rose said to the group with a beaming smile.

Rose's cornflower-blue eyes sparkled in the lamp light and Jared was entranced by her gentle voice yet again.

'Shut yer mouth, Jared, there's a tram coming,' Dan whispered.

Jared's jaws clamped shut, his teeth making a loud crack, and he flushed with embarrassment when the others burst out laughing.

Jared Johnson might have thought he was in love before – but now he *knew* he was.

20

'Rose is coming back to the Unicorn, she's staying the night,' Judith informed them, then to her friend said, 'Dad will be so pleased to see you.'

'I'll get my coat and meet you outside,' Rose answered.

Jared's heart skipped a beat as she smiled at him. As they made their way through the throng of people standing around exchanging gossip, Jared's mind again turned to Clarice.

On first meeting Clarice, Jared had been shy and his heart had hammered. But when he met Rose, he felt like he'd been pole-axed. She had taken his breath away and his blood was on fire as it rushed through his veins. She had gone but a minute and he felt bereft; a physical pain in his chest threatening to bring him to his knees.

Pushing through the doors, Jared drew in a great lungful of air, the coldness enabling him to breathe easier. He had let Clarice slip away from him and he was glad of it after the way she had treated him. But he had no intention of losing Rose.

A sudden thought brought him up sharply. What if she already had a sweetheart? *Please, God, don't let that be!*

'Judith,' he said quietly, 'does Rose... is she...?'

'No, she doesn't and no, she's not,' Judith answered with a grin. She knew he was asking if her friend was attached and she saw the relief flood his face.

'Hey up, I do believe our Jared has been hit by Cupid's arrow,' Johnny joked.

'I'm not surprised, Rose is rather lovely,' Paul put in.

'I think we might have to stand in line,' Dan added.

'Give over, you lot,' Jared said but he too grinned widely.

'I'm sorry I kept you, but I was arranging my next performance for tomorrow night whilst I removed my stage make-up,' Rose said as she hurried towards the group.

Jared thought she was even lovelier without all the make-up. Her skin was clear and fresh and her smile could light up a room. Her eyes sparkled in the light spilling from the theatre doorway as they met his. Jared's stomach flipped and he felt sure he had a silly grin on his face but he could do nothing about it.

'I think we should get you ladies home safe and sound,' Seth said as Judith slid her arm through his.

Jared immediately fell in step with Rose and struck up a conversation. The others tagged behind, exchanging smiles and nudges as they watched their boss work his magic on the young singer.

All the way back to the Unicorn, Jared and Rose talked, completely at ease with one another. There were no awkward pauses and it was as though they had known each other for years.

Seth held open the door as everyone trooped into the bar but they stopped dead in their tracks when they saw Joe Kingston wielding a cosh at two arguing men. The sight of the weapon brought the disagreement to a halt in double quick time.

When Joe caught sight of Judith and Rose, he replaced the

cosh behind the bar and held out his arms. Rose rushed to him and was enveloped in his loving embrace.

A twinge of jealousy hit Jared and he was momentarily taken aback. *Don't be stupid*, he told himself, *she's not your sweetheart yet.*

Seth ordered their beers, served by Pokey, and watched the reunion.

There were whistles from the patrons and Joe lifted the cosh once more, but his smile belied his action.

'Rose is staying over, Dad,' Judith called out over the hubbub in the room.

'Very good,' Joe replied before his attention was drawn to a waiting customer, and Rose returned to the group.

'We should go on up to bed,' Judith said. 'Thanks for taking me tonight.' Her comment was aimed at all of them, then to Seth she added, 'I'll see you tomorrow night.'

'Rose, before you go up, may I have a quiet word?' Jared said quickly. The two moved a few steps away, not noticing the grins of the others.

Feeling flustered, Jared looked down at his boots, trying to find the right words. When he looked up again, Rose gave him an encouraging smile.

'I know you're busy what with singing at the theatre and all but...' Jared faltered. He felt as if his tongue had swollen to twice its normal size.

'But...?' Rose said.

'Well, I was wondering if perhaps... if you can find time, that is, you would come to dinner with me tomorrow night – or maybe supper after your show?' Jared's words came out in a rush before he completely lost his nerve.

'Supper would be lovely, thank you. If you come to the

Palace, I'll tell the staff you're with me and they'll let you in for free. You can wait backstage until I've finished.'

'Thanks, I'll look forward to it,' Jared said. He was relieved that she had consented to walk out with him.

'Me too.'

Wandering back to the group, they said goodnight to the ladies. Then the banter began.

Jared suffered their teasing all the way homeward, and when they stopped to part ways, Sam thanked his friends. 'It was just what I needed.'

'Will you be all right?' Jared asked.

Sam nodded. 'Yes, I'll see you all in the morning.'

'You coming back to work?' Tom asked.

'It's better than moping at home,' Sam replied.

'Good on yer,' Paul said, clapping him on the back.

The boys went on their way and Seth and Jared walked home together, chatting quietly. The wind rushed through the streets with an eldritch moan and the boys hunched their heads down into their shoulders. Once indoors, they made tea and had bread, cheese and ham for supper in the kitchen.

'I'm going to ask for Judith's hand,' Seth said all of a sudden.

Jared spat out his tea and began to cough. 'Already?' he asked as he brushed the droplets from his jersey. 'You've only known her for two minutes.'

'I know, but life is for living, mate. We could all be dead tomorrow and I'll kick myself if I miss this chance.'

'I can't argue with that,' Jared said. 'Good luck to you.'

'And to you with Rose,' Seth answered.

Clinking cups, the two drank their tea in silence, each lost in their own thoughts about their ladies.

* * *

Whilst Jared had been meeting Rose Whitman, Clarice and Clifford had gone on to yet another gambling house. As usual, they had eaten first and Clarice had again negotiated her way around ordering her food. A little wine had been consumed then, as they sat digesting their dinners, Clifford had said, 'Clara, you are positively the most beautiful woman I have ever seen.'

No blush followed Clarice's sweet smile, but she played the coy maiden to perfection.

'Do you realise you have stolen my heart?' Clifford asked.

Clarice's eyes looked up as she sipped her drink. What could she say to that? She knew he had fallen hard for her but she didn't feel the same way. Replacing her glass on the table, she took a breath and replied, 'I do, sweetheart, and I'm very fond of you.' With a tight smile, she thought, *Clarice, is there no end to your lies?*

Clifford beamed his pleasure and, finishing their wine, they left the restaurant.

In the casino at last, Clarice was glad to know where they were so she could visit any time. She had money to accrue and this was the easiest way of doing it.

Clifford rarely gambled now, he was content to watch his Clara play and win. At one time, he and his friend, Anthony Purcell, had frequented the casinos often and enjoyed their gambling evenings, but since Clifford had met Clara, his interest in the cards had waned. He simply could not take his eyes off her and was happy to stand behind her with his hand on her shoulder. It was not a sign to others that she belonged to him, it was more that it was the only way he could be so close to her. He breathed in her scent, felt the warmth of her body and heard her laugh as she won yet another round.

Clarice, aka Clara, wasn't bothered either way how Clifford

felt about her. As long as he kept introducing her to these clubs, she was happy enough.

Immediately Clarice settled herself at the card table and with Clifford taking his usual place at her back, the games began.

The gentlemen around the table were dressed in sombre black suits, their fob watches attached securely to Albert chains tucked neatly into waistcoat pockets. White shirts had stiff collars held in place by studs and one or two had a flower pinned to a lapel, looking for all the world like they were attending a wedding. Glasses of whisky sat on the tables next to the cards and were gulped from every now and then.

Clarice glanced around the room and at the high ceiling where shadows lurked. Gas lamps lit up the playing areas and the tables were separated by wide spaces to allow players some privacy. The décor was dated but clean and carpets muffled footsteps as people walked from room to room. There was a lot of noise; men shouting encouragement in the corner where a dice game was in full swing. Waitresses wove their way around the room delivering drinks and smiling their thanks for tips given.

As was her wont, Clarice won more than she lost, graciously accepting the praise of the other players. She was adept at most card games and moved from one table to another throughout the evening.

It was around two o'clock in the morning when she finally stood to leave. Giving her thanks to the gamers, she and Clifford left the club. He hailed a cab and as they travelled, he suggested they have a day at the races and Clarice agreed readily. It would mean stepping up a rung on the social ladder, and she would at last be mixing with the upper class. Her coffers were swelling nicely and she decided it was time to actually move from the boarding house and into the Midland Hotel. If she was to be sharing time with the toffs, she could no longer be skulking through the streets late at night to get home. Her mind made up, she determined she would move the very next day and would stay there as long as her luck held at playing cards.

One more night at the boarding house and then she would be a woman of means, her abode reflecting her status.

So consumed with her thoughts was she that when Clifford spoke again, she was rather taken aback.

'Darling, it's time we got to know each other a little more – intimately, don't you think?'

Recovering her composure quickly, she snapped, 'Clifford! What do you take me for?'

'Sweetheart, I just meant...' he faltered.

'I know exactly what you meant and I'm shocked!' Clarice covered her mouth with a gloved hand to forestall the words she really wanted to say which were, *And you can bugger off, you dirty old lecher!*

'I'm sorry, please don't be angry with me. I can't bear it,' Clifford pleaded.

'You must understand that a lady holds on to her virtue until she is married,' Clarice said quietly.

'I do! It's simply that I adore you, Clara, and I want us to be together – in every way.'

'I'm sure, but it's not to be, Clifford. I would not even entertain the idea until my wedding night.' Clarice was careful not to say *until we are wed.*

'Fair enough, please forgive me,' Clifford said sulkily.

'I will, provided you don't raise the subject again.' Satisfied when he grumbled his agreement, Clarice sat in silence for the rest of the journey.

You start thinking like that, my lad, and you'll have to go! The words tripped through her mind and then she added, *I don't really need you now anyway.*

She did, however, keep him at arm's length, allowing only a peck on the cheek when they parted in the early hours of the morning.

21

The following day passed interminably slowly for Jared. He wished the hours away so he could be with Rose again, and he found it impossible to concentrate on anything other than her. Images of her floated in his mind and his stomach did somersaults. He ate his breakfast and lunch like an automaton, tasting nothing as he chewed and swallowed. His eyes constantly flicked to the tin clock on the wall, which only made things worse, as time appeared to stand still.

Eventually the rattle of cartwheels heralded the return of the tatters and Jared was out of his seat and out of the office like a whippet. He stood impatiently tapping his foot as the horses were released from their traces and led back to the stables. He watched as the bundles were thrown from the carts and piled up, ready for sorting the next day. Pacing back and forth, he knew this last hour of the business day would drag by and seem endless.

At last, the yard emptied of people and the braziers were made safe outside the building. Jared swiftly locked up and led his friends in a rapid pace homeward. Of course, they were all aware of his seeing Rose later and again the jests rang out. Jared took it all in good sport, especially when Johnny asked, 'You surely won't be having a bath every night?'

'He won't, it's too bloody expensive!' Seth countered. Having to burn wood and coal to heat the water was indeed a drain on the finances, hence most of the population only bathing once a week or even once a fortnight.

'Put some clean underdrawers on as well,' Dan said with a grin.

'Why?' Jared asked.

'In case you get knocked down; you wouldn't want the nurse at the hospital seeing you in dirty underwear!' Sam said innocently, much to the amusement of his friends. 'That's what my mum always told me.'

Seeing the sadness cross the boy's face by the light of the moon, Jared replied, 'That's good advice, Sam, thanks.'

Once home, Seth and Jared prepared a meal then Jared had a strip wash and donned his best clothes.

'Very smart,' Seth said after he had done the same. His evenings were now taken up at the Unicorn where he could spend time with Judith once her shift behind the bar ended.

When Seth had gone, Jared was left behind, wondering what to do with his time before he too could go to see his girl. *His girl!* The thought made him smile. She must be keen on him too because hadn't she readily accepted his invitation to supper? With her looks and personality, Rose must have had lots of offers and he pushed aside this thought. He didn't want to know whether she had accepted any of them as well.

Glancing at the clock, Jared had two hours to kill before he could go to the Palace, so he decided it was the perfect opportunity to run an errand he'd been putting off. Locking the house securely, Jared strode out across the heath. The streets were dimly lit by gas lamps, casting small pools of yellow light inter-spersed by patches of dark shadow. It was quieter now as most folk were home from their work, but there were early revellers abroad, some already too drunk to stand. One fellow danced a jig to a tune only he could hear, and another was bent double in an alley, his stomach and beer parting company noisily.

At last Jared arrived at his destination and knocked on the door. A few seconds later, a voice greeted him. 'Jared!'

'Hello, Mr Connaught, I wonder if I may have a moment of your time.'

'Come in,' John said, 'through there.' He pointed to a doorway which led into a small but clean living room. 'Take a seat, lad, tea?'

'No, thanks.'

John sat in his own armchair opposite Jared by the fire. 'This is a surprise. What can I do for you?'

'Nothing, Mr—'

'John.'

'I came to tell you I saw Clarice last night,' Jared said, getting straight to the point.

John nodded and Jared noted there was no trace of the excitement on the man's face that he had expected to see.

'She was with a man at the Gaiety Palace – a toff,' Jared went on.

Still John didn't speak, so Jared ploughed on. 'I spoke to her but she pretended not to know me, so I walked away. They left early and I have no idea where they went.'

After a long silence, John said, 'I tried to tell you what she was like but I'm not sure you believed me.'

Jared rubbed a hand across his mouth, knowing the man was right.

'I'm sorry, Jared, but in a way it's a good thing it happened.'

'How so?'

'Now you can get her out of your system. I think you liked my daughter, maybe enough to walk out with her.'

'I thought so at the time, but I've met someone who I think I'd like to spend the rest of my life with.' Jared couldn't believe the words coming from his mouth so openly.

'Then I wish you all the best, lad, and hope you grow old together,' John said wistfully.

'Will you try to find her – Clarice, I mean?' Jared asked.

'No. There would be no point in dragging her back here only for her to run away again. She has made her bed, now she must lie in it. Besides, from what you've told me, it seems she's landed on her feet. It's the gent I feel sorry for.' John shook his head as he looked Jared directly in the eye. When he saw a frown crease Jared's face, he went on, 'Clarice will use that man to get what she wants then she'll throw him away like an old dishcloth.'

'Surely she wouldn't be so callous?'

John's eyebrows shot up. 'She snubbed you, didn't she? A callous action to my mind.'

'My pals thought the same and to be honest so did I.'

'There you go then.' John spread his hands before replacing them on the arms of the chair.

'Maybe I shouldn't have come to tell you—'

'I'm glad you did, son,' John cut across, 'at least now I know she's come to no harm.'

Jared's head rocked up and down slowly as he considered the words.

'Will you take that tea now?' John asked.

'Thanks, I believe I will,' Jared replied with a smile.

22

Clarice had busied herself moving out of the boarding house and into a room at the Midland Hotel. As she unpacked her clothes and hung them in the wardrobe, she smiled to herself. One step at a time, she had made her way from the working class, living in what she deemed a hovel, to residing in a posh hotel. Glancing around, she took in the chintz curtains and Tiffany-style bedside lamp. A comfortable bed, a wardrobe and dressing table to match, there was also a washstand on top of which sat a large jug and bowl set. A small armchair was placed near the fireplace. There was a faint odour of soot in the air; clearly the chimney had recently been swept. Clarice opened the window and a blast of cold air rushed through, once the smell had gone, she closed it again. The bed sheets were pristine white and the blankets fawn-coloured wool. There were two pillows which were well stuffed with feathers. Looking like it was painted by a child, a picture of a poppy hung on the wall; it was rather quaint.

The hotel, situated on Stephenson Street, was wedged close to the bank on one side and on the other was Burlington Passage which was not much more than an alleyway. Standing behind New Street railway station, Clarice thought it might be noisy in the daytime with steam trains coming and going. However, she was not perturbed by this as she had no intention of being in her room at that time. No, Clarice would be spending the daylight hours playing cards at one or another of the numerous gambling houses she was swiftly learning about.

Sitting on her bed, Clarice again counted her money. She had paid for a month's stay up front at the hotel which had eaten into her coffers, but which she could soon replenish with a good visit to the tables. The next thing on her agenda was to discover where other casinos were so she could spread her time across a wide range of them.

Pleased she had enough money to be going on with, Clarice considered spending the afternoon at one of the gambling houses then dismissed the idea. She would be seeing Clifford later so they could go together. Having laid out her clothes in readiness for her evening out, Clarice paced her room, boredom creeping in, followed quickly by frustration. She wanted to go and play cards – no, she *needed* to.

Donning her coat, she then pinned her dark blue hat in place and grabbing her bag she left the room. Nodding to the receptionist, she stepped outside to hail a cab.

Calling out her destination, Clarice climbed aboard and instantly felt better. Excitement coursed through her body which she tried to temper by looking out of the window.

Hordes of people pushed and shoved their way along the streets, all eager to be somewhere. A few of the more wealthy stood out amongst the crowds of the poor. Shabbily dressed women in their old coats and even older hats bustled along with their unkempt children. Men in patched jackets and trousers, mufflers tied about their necks and wearing dirty flat caps hung around on street corners in the bread line. In stark contrast, gentlemen in their well-cut knee-length coats, top hats and carrying silver-topped canes paraded. By their sides walked ladies dressed in the most up-to-date fashions in bright blues or reds. Their hats were large and fussy, covered in silk flowers; dainty shoes peeping from beneath the hems of their long skirts. Clearly these women shopped in the very best places, most likely in London, as opposed to the market.

I'll shop in London one day, Clarice thought as the cab rattled along.

The weather was gloomy and grey and Clarice was glad she would be spending the next few hours indoors doing something she loved.

The cab drew to a halt outside Monty's, named after its owner, Monty Sherbourne, a very rich industrialist hailing from Manchester, and Clarice alighted. Paying the cabbie, she rapped on the door.

'Ah, hello again, Miss Christian.'

Clarice was surprised the doorman remembered her name but she smiled sweetly. 'Hello, Silas,' she said in response.

'Please come in, your table awaits.'

Clarice stepped over the threshold and followed Silas's large frame as he walked towards the gaming room. White teeth glinted through his dark beard and moustache as he smiled when he led her to her preferred table.

Clarice pulled a coin from her bag and passed it to Silas by way of thanks and the man beamed with pleasure.

'Good luck,' he whispered in her ear before he strode back to his place at the front door.

Clarice greeted the men around the table, some of whom she had met before, and the game began. A few hands of cards here, then she might move to play another table.

After winning a couple of times, Clarice moved to the baccarat table. Taking a seat, she nodded as the game began; the object being to assemble a hand of two or three cards where a point value is nine or as close to nine as the player can get. Then she strolled over to play whist. Ordering coffee from a passing waitress, she returned the girl's smile before settling down to play. Her coffee arrived and Clarice dropped a small chip on the tray, receiving a, 'Thank you, ma'am,' in response. Nodding, she turned back to the game, saying, 'Gentlemen, shall we begin?'

Clarice thoroughly enjoyed her afternoon's sport and reluctantly stood to leave. It was time to go and ready herself for when Clifford arrived. Then, after blagging her way through a menu she couldn't read, she would be back to feel the thrill of gambling once more.

On the journey home, Clarice felt moody, already missing the feel of the cards in her hand.

Back in her room, she rushed to change her clothes and checked her look in the mirror. A little rouge on her cheekbones and she was ready. Taking the stairs sedately, she walked with her head held high to the foyer, then pulled on her gloves, having stepped through the door. Clifford arrived right on time and helped her into the waiting cab.

On the way to the restaurant, Clifford asked, 'Clara, m'dear, how was your day?'

'Fine, Clifford, and yours?'

'Oh, you know, did a little business on the pater's behalf, lunch with the boys and afternoon tea with Mama.'

It's all right for some! Clarice kept her tongue behind her teeth and forced a smile.

'How did you fill your time, sweetheart?' Clifford pushed.

Clarice wanted to tell him to shut the hell up, but she

answered, 'A little of this and that.' Abruptly she changed the subject with, 'Where are we off to tonight?'

'I thought the theatre, there's a splendid play on I'd rather like to see.'

Curling her lip in the darkness of the cab, Clarice wanted to scream out her frustration. Instead she just murmured, 'Hmm.' Who on earth would want to watch a fusty old play when they could be having fun in a casino?

Clarice looked out of the window as she focused her attention on how to get out of going to the theatre.

Way across town, Clarice and Clifford had dined well and as they left the restaurant, Clarice said, 'Would you mind awfully if we didn't go to the theatre?'

'Oh, I... was rather looking forward to the play,' Clifford muttered.

'Then you should go. I think I could do with an early night anyway.'

'If you're sure, m'dear?'

'Yes, the rest will do me good.'

The cab took them back to the Midland Hotel, where Clifford kissed her cheek then set off to watch the play.

Clarice didn't even step inside the hotel, she merely turned and hailed another cab.

'Monty's, please,' she said before boarding. The cab pulled away and Clarice smiled into the darkness. *Bugger going to the theatre, there's fun to be had and money to be won!*

23

After taking tea with John Connaught, Jared hot-footed it round to the Gaiety Palace where he was led into the wings to watch Rose sing. His heart soared as she waved to him from the opposite side of the stage before she went on. He waved back and spontaneously blew her a kiss; he thought he would burst with joy as he caught the kiss she sent back to him.

The applause and stamping of feet slowed to a hush as Rose took up her position. The band started up and silence reigned as Rose sang 'If You Were Only Mine'. The crowd went wild when she finished and flowers flew onto the stage to land at her feet.

Jared laughed when she called out, 'If you're going to give me flowers, I'd best sing another!' Whistles and cheers filled the room and again Rose sang, this time, 'Silver Threads Among the Gold'. On she went, finishing with 'Little Brown Jug', where she encouraged the audience to join in. Finally she gathered up her flowers, waved to the audience, took a bow and ran offstage, straight into Jared's arms.

'You were amazing,' he said breathlessly.

'Give me five minutes to get changed and take off my stage make-up and I'll be with you,' Rose answered with a smile.

Jared nodded and as she skipped away he turned to watch the juggler being pelted with bits of food. The boos and hisses left the poor man in no doubt his performance was not being appreciated. Gathering his fallen clubs, he raced into the wings.

'Bloody animals out there tonight!' he said as he strode past Jared.

Next came the mime artist in white face paint and striped jersey. Even Jared had to admit that the acts were less than entertaining as cat-calls sent the man running for safety.

Then the Lion Comique strolled the boards, a man dressed as a toff who sang about drinking champagne, going to the races, womanising and gambling; the audience appeared to be enjoying his performance at least.

With his hands in his pockets, Jared tapped his foot in time with the music.

'I'm ready,' a silky voice whispered quietly behind him and as Jared turned, he was certain he was looking at an angel.

'Are you hungry?' he asked.

'Famished!' Rose replied.

'Right, let's get you fed then.' Jared hooked an elbow and warmth spread throughout him as Rose slipped her arm through his.

Leaving the Palace, the couple chatted as they walked briskly to the small restaurant Jared had decided upon. Holding open the door for Rose to enter first, Jared asked for a cosy table in the corner. Although quite late, the place was humming with activity. Theatre goers and folk just out to eat filled the room all talking and laughing. The lighting was subdued and pristine white linen adorned the tables, giving the whole place a pleasant and happy atmosphere.

Once they were seated, Jared ordered wine and the two gazed at the menu cards. Because the restaurant was a small family-run eating house, the choices were limited, but it was all good fresh food.

'What do you fancy?' Jared asked.

'Shepherd's pie and cabbage,' Rose replied.

Jared nodded in agreement. 'Me too.'

Their wine was poured, their order taken and Jared raised his glass. 'To many more evenings like this.'

They clinked glasses. 'Cheers,' Rose said.

Between bites of deliciously hot food, Rose told Jared a little of her life story.

'My family – Mum, Dad and my brother – live in Wednesbury. They moved 'cos my dad got a job there, he's the manager at a nail factory. I didn't want to go so I stayed in the house and got work at the Palace. It doesn't pay much but I can manage if I'm careful with my money. Dad owns the house, so I don't have to pay rent.'

Jared then related how his mum and sister had died years ago. His father had spent eight years in jail after swinging a punch, missing his intended victim and catching a policeman on the jaw. Tim Johnson now worked at the yard as a sorter and father and son were reunited at last.

They discussed the acts put on at the Palace; jugglers, comics, singers, dancers, knife throwers, even a man who said his dog could sing! Rose explained how much she loved life at the theatre.

'I could see that from how you interacted with the audience,' Jared commented.

'Mostly they're very kind,' she replied, 'to me they are anyway. Although some of the acts do go through the mill sometimes like the juggler did tonight.'

'I hate to say it, but he wasn't very good. He kept dropping his clubs.'

'I know and the worst of it is, he doesn't get any better. I'm afraid by the end of the week he could find himself out of work. I hate the thought that his wife and child will go hungry if he gets the sack.'

'Maybe it's time for him to find a different trade,' Jared said, not unkindly.

In what felt like no time at all, Jared realised they were the only two left in the dining room and the waiter was sitting at a table with his chin in his hand, clearly tired to the bone.

'I think I should pay the bill and let that poor fellow get to his bed,' Jared said.

The couple left arm in arm, both bundled up against the falling temperature. They strolled along, oblivious of everything around them, just glad to be in each other's company. Happy drunks were passed by unnoticed, rattling cartwheels unheard and the cold unfelt; Jared and Rose were in their own little world.

'This is it,' Rose said as she drew him to a halt outside a terraced house which stood in shadow between two gas street lamps.

'Tomorrow?' Jared asked tentatively, praying she'd enjoyed herself and would agree to see him again.

'Yes. Will you come to the Palace for me?'

'Wild horses couldn't stop me!' Jared said before he tried to gather her up in his arms in order to kiss her.

Rose held up her hand, saying, 'Let's take this slowly. I like you very much, Jared, but be patient with me.'

'I'm sorry, oh, God, I feel like such a fool!' Jared said, dropping his arms to his sides. 'It's just that...'

'I know, I understand how you feel but we should get to know each other better, don't you think?'

'Yes, yes, of course. Rose, I'm so very sorry, please don't hold it against me.'

With a tinkling laugh, she said, 'I promise I won't.'

Jared felt much better. 'I'll say goodnight then.'

'Goodnight. I'll see you tomorrow.'

Jared was about to turn away when Rose stepped towards him and planted a quick kiss on his cheek before turning and walking indoors.

Jared thought he'd died and gone to heaven.

24

Jared was feeling rather sad as he walked over to Sam's house in Bromley Street. He had bought a dark suit for the occasion and was a little uncomfortable in it. He was much more used to being in old trousers and jacket for his work.

He knocked the door and waited for Sam to answer.

'You look smart,' Jared said, glancing over Sam's black suit and polished shoes.

'Thanks, Mum says...' The words were cut off by a sob catching in his throat.

'My mum used to say the same, always be nicely turned out on special occasions,' Jared said, feeling sad for himself as well as his friend.

'Jared, I'm an orphan now.' It was as if the realisation had only just hit Sam and he dropped into an armchair.

'I thought I was for years, so I know exactly how you feel.' Jared knew that no amount of comforting words would make Sam feel any better today. It was Friday, the day of Mrs Jenkins's funeral.

One by one, the others arrived, all looking dapper in their

funereal garb. Paul, Dan, Tom, Johnny and Seth were all here to support their friend through the most difficult time of his life by walking with him behind the funeral carriage. Everyone else, including Toby and Alice McGuire, the Cavenor brothers, sorters and grooms, would be waiting at the church.

There was a sharp rap on the door and Sam jumped to his feet. 'Here we go.'

The hearse, pulled by four black horses, stood outside. As the equines pawed the ground, eager to be moving, their feather plumes began to flutter. The casket lay on the cart with a single wreath of flowers on the lid, fastened down with strong string against the wind attempting to carry it off.

At the side of the doorway stood the conductor, his top hat resting on his folded arm, the other loose by his side. He nodded at Sam's greeting and led them all to their positions behind the cart where they would walk sedately. The conductor then replaced his topper and strode ahead to lead the cortege to St Bartholomew's.

As they processed into Heath Mill Lane, bystanders watched sombrely. Women crossed themselves and men held their flat caps over their chests as a sign of respect. Snotty-nosed children stood with their fingers in their mouths, watching with wonder.

Turning into Fazeley Street, they walked on to pass beneath the viaduct before entering Park Street Gardens.

Jared thought it a nice touch that the funeral director had chosen this route rather than fight through the traffic of the Bull Ring.

People enjoying the gardens stopped to pay their respects, top hats and bowlers raised as the coffin passed by. Ladies out riding pulled their horses to a standstill as the procession moved on.

The cortege stopped at the church where four pall-bearers

gently lifted the casket onto their shoulders and carried it indoors where they laid it with reverence on a bier.

Sam and the others followed and took their places in the front pews as the pall-bearers retreated to wait at the back of the church.

The vicar began the service and Jared noticed Sam staring at the coffin. *He's saying a last private goodbye*, he thought. Glancing around, he saw lots of people, neighbours and friends, he supposed. Some were dressed traditionally in dark colours, others came in whatever they had to hand that was clean and tidy. The women had pulled out their best hats and the few men there held their caps in their hands. A baby cried at the back of the church and as the sobs faded Jared realised the lady had taken the child outside rather than disrupt the service. Jared's attention was quickly drawn back to Sam when he heard a strangled sob. Placing a hand on his friend's shoulder, he gave a gentle squeeze. It was Jared's way of saying *we're all here for you, mate*. Sam glanced at him and nodded his thanks.

Then, with the close of the service, the pall-bearers appeared once more to carry the coffin to its final resting place in the graveyard. Once more, the conductor led and Sam, his friends and the rest of the mourners followed behind.

Laying the coffin over the ropes which would be used to lower it into the ground, the pall-bearers stood in stony silence.

The vicar's words were lost on Sam, who stared vacantly. Jared had to nudge him to lead the tossing of a handful of dirt onto the coffin lid once it was in its grave.

One by one, everyone shook the vicar's hand and slowly wandered away from the churchyard.

Toby McGuire and his wife came to say goodbye to Sam and the others. 'It was a nice service, to be sure.'

'Thanks for coming, Mr McGuire, you too, Mrs McGuire,' Sam said sorrowfully.

Alice threw her arms around the young man and gave him a big hug and when she let him go, he gave her a little smile.

'If you need anything, lad, just send word.' Toby shook the boy's hand and they turned and left the cemetery.

'Where's the wake, Sam?' Johnny asked as gently as he could.

'There isn't one – I couldn't afford it,' Sam answered simply.

The lads exchanged a sad look then Jared said, 'All back to the Unicorn then.'

Sam gave him a grateful smile as they turned towards their destination. Serious drinking time was awasting.

Judith and her father were surprised to see the coterie at that time of day and all dressed in black, no less. Seth was quick to appraise her of the situation and she said for a small remuneration she would be happy to provide a funeral tea. At his nod, she disappeared into the kitchen to request the cook cut some sandwiches and sort out a salad bowl along with some cake. It was the best she could do on such short notice.

In the meantime, Seth surreptitiously had a whip-round to pay for it, careful not to let Sam know what they were about, whilst Jared bought a round of beers and kept Sam busy passing them out. It would be the first of many and most, if not all, would suffer the after effects the following morning. However, Jared and the others were ensuring Mrs Jenkins had a right good send-off.

By five o'clock, Sam was rip-roaring drunk, one minute laughing and shouting, the next in a paroxysm of tears.

Jared decided it would be best to stay reasonably sober – someone had to get this lot home, after all. Leaning on the bar counter, he watched the revelry. Johnny and Paul were having an arm-wrestling match, the old-timers in the pub cheering them on with added bits of advice thrown in for good measure. Sam and Tom were endeavouring to dance a jig to the accompaniment of an Irish navvy's surprisingly good singing. Seth was trying to find a canoodling moment with Judith, who was rushed off her feet, and Dan was having a good-natured debate with an old farmer about horses.

'Bloody hell, look at 'em!' Tim Johnson said as he sidled towards his son.

'I know, Dad, and I've got to get them home somehow.'

'I'll help and Seth is too busy with his girl to be drinking so we may have another there to aid our endeavour.'

'I live in hope,' Jared said with a grin.

'I'm so proud of you, son, I don't tell you often enough,' Tim said. Jared blushed as he sipped his ale. 'These blokes think the world of you, as do I. I wish your mum was here to see how you've turned out.'

'Me too. I miss her and our Maisy, especially at times like these.' Jared felt the familiar stab of pain as always when he thought of his loss. Now his friend would be suffering the same, but possibly not right at that moment, for just then Sam's legs plaited and he went down hard. Jared shook his head as, undeterred, Sam got up and tried again.

'This was a good idea, lad, Sam will always remember what you did for him.'

'Are you sure?' Jared said with a smile as he tilted his head towards the young man trying to dance and drink at the same time.

Father and son laughed loudly as Sam called for another beer.

'How's that lass of yours?' Tim asked out of the blue.

'Rose. She's marvellous.'

'Serious then, is it?'

'Yes, I think it is, Dad. I'd be happy for us to grow old together. I love the very bones of her.'

'When you know – you know,' Tim said quietly.

'Was it like that with you and Mum?'

'Yes, lad, it was.'

The two shared a knowing smile and continued to watch the others having a rollicking good time.

25

Clarice was amassing a tidy sum with her visits to the different gambling houses. Not nearly enough to live in luxury or even call herself rich, but she was getting there. All she had to do was to keep winning.

With a forced smile to the aged gent at the table, Clarice shrugged at losing the hand. She counted her few chips and shook her head.

'Never mind, dear, perhaps the next round will be luckier for you,' the gentleman said.

'I hope so, I'm running out of these.' Clarice gently ran a manicured hand over the counters.

The dealer gave her a look which said, *I know what you're up to – poor little me! You're hoping he'll give you a few chips to play with.*

Clarice ignored him and the hand began. She fully intended to win this one so she could silently thumb her nose at the arrogant dealer.

'Oh, well done!' exclaimed the gent as Clarice raked in all of the pot and began to pile up her winnings. With a grin, she gave her thanks; to the dealer she raised an eyebrow. The man surreptitiously inclined his head a mere fraction. The two now had an understanding; he knew she could play bloody good cards, and she was onto his snot-nosed attitude.

By the time she was ready to cash in her chips, Clarice was tired to the bone. Tossing a token to the dealer, which would ensure he stayed onside, Clarice said her goodnights.

At the door, a line of cabs were waiting, they had quickly learned they would receive good tips from those leaving in the early hours of the morning.

Opening a cab door, Clarice called out, 'Midland Hotel, please.'

'Right away, missus,' the cabbie said, knuckling his forehead.

Clarice settled back as her journey began. The streets were quiet with all God-fearing people in their beds. In the distance, a church bell chimed four times. Clarice was surprised, she hadn't realised how long she'd been playing – no wonder she was weary. A dog started to bark but after a yelp it was silenced again. The sound of the horse's hooves on the cobbles echoed loudly in the dark streets and the cold invaded Clarice's coat.

The cab halted and Clarice paid the cabbie and gave a large gratuity. Tipping his hat, he went on his way. *He'll probably join the back of the line again. What a rotten job in the bad weather*, Clarice thought as she watched him go.

Entering the hotel, Clarice went to her room, making as little noise as possible. She didn't want to disturb other guests who might complain and get her thrown out.

She was delighted that someone had lit a fire in her room and it was cosy and warm. It had burned down, with only a few embers glowing stubbornly in the bottom of the grate. Clarice threw on a few nuggets of coal from the scuttle standing on the hearth, along with a couple of sticks to help it along. Seeing a tiny flame appear, she blew on it and, satisfied it was burning again, she began to ready herself for bed.

Dressed in her voluminous cotton nightdress with a thick woollen shawl around her shoulders, Clarice sat in the armchair, watching the fire lick around the coals. It was like seeing a ballet, the yellow dancing flames were mesmerising and Clarice felt all her tension drain away. Her eyelids started to droop so she put the guard in place and climbed into bed.

Her last thought before sleep claimed her was, *I really must not spend so much time in the gambling houses.*

* * *

Most sensible people were tucked up in their beds at the time Jared, Tim and Seth rounded up the lads when Joe Kingston called, 'Time, gentlemen, please!' He rang an old bell hanging over the bar then went about collecting glasses.

Arm in arm, in a line, the men wobbled their way down the street. Jared guessed the cabbies wouldn't entertain transporting lads who were three sheets to the wind, lest they threw up in the carriage. So Shanks's Pony it was and laughter and song echoed through the mostly deserted streets.

One by one, they were escorted home by their minders. Then they arrived at Sam's. The house was in darkness and Sam stood and stared. 'Mum always waited up for me,' he muttered, trying his best to stand still. His head began to nod of its own accord and he staggered sideways. Looking down, he took a breath and planted his feet a stride apart. With a satisfied grin that he'd won control over at least one part of his body, Sam raised his eyes to the house again. 'I've got a key here somewhere,' he said, patting his pockets.

Jared and Tim exchanged a smirk at Sam's antics then Jared

helped locate the key and let Sam indoors. 'Will you be all right? You can come and stay at ours if you want,' Jared said from where they stood on the street.

With a slow shake of his head, Sam slurred, 'I'll be fine, thanksh, mates.' With that, he kicked the door shut.

Seth, Jared and Tim burst out laughing when they heard a crash and Sam shout, 'Who put that bloody table there?'

The three chatted quietly as they made for home. 'I wonder how many will turn in for work in the morning?' Tim asked.

'God knows. I'll see how they are and if they look a bit green, I'll send them home.'

Tim said goodnight and went his own way and Jared and Seth wandered down Watery Lane before crossing onto the heath. Jared couldn't help casting a glance at the house he'd once shared with his mum and sister.

'I'm ready for some supper and a cup of tea,' Seth said as they reached their home.

'Me too. Fancy sausage and onions on some bread and butter?'

'You bet!'

'Right, I'll cook – you brew,' Jared said as they walked indoors. Lighting the oil lamp, he went to fetch the sausages from the cold slab.

As they ate, they discussed their lady-loves. 'I'm gonna ask Judith to marry me,' Seth said all of a sudden.

Jared choked on his sandwich and began to cough. After a sip of tea, he answered, 'You keep doing that to me! Anyway, it's a little quick, isn't it? I mean, you've only known her for a short while.'

'I know but I'm going mad not being able to be with her. She's all I think about.'

Jared knew what he meant because he felt exactly the same about Rose. 'Well, if you're sure...'

'I am. I'm gonna talk to Joe about it tomorrow night.'

'Then I wish you good luck,' Jared said as he washed their dishes.

'Ta, pal. I'll see you in the morning.'

Jared watched his friend go up the stairs, then he sat in front of the range, its doors open and the heat spilling out to warm the kitchen. He considered Seth's words again and before long he was imagining what it would be like being wed to Rose.

A smile spread across his face as he pictured them in marital bliss. Jared closed his eyes and allowed his mind to show him the moving images of a wedding firstly, then children and grandchildren, before two old people sat together on the sofa holding hands.

Getting to his feet, he shut the range doors, locked up and doused the lights. Climbing the stairs, he knew that the scenario he had just envisaged was what he wanted and, like Seth, the sooner the better.

26

Jared had confided in his employer about the state of affairs with Clarice; how she'd just upped and left and then how she had rebuffed him in the queue at the Gaiety Palace.

'That tells you what sort she is, so it does,' Toby said.

'I suppose so. I have to admit it hurt my feelings. Even if she'd just said *hello, Jared* it wouldn't have been so bad.'

'Social climber, sounds like,' Toby added.

'That's what the lads said.'

'Ah, but now you've met someone new, is that right?' Toby asked with a grin.

Jared laughed as he told of meeting Rose and how he now knew how Toby felt about Alice.

'I hope you don't make the mistakes I made, lad,' Toby said quietly. 'If this lady is for you, then don't let her get away.'

'I don't intend to, Mr McGuire. She said she wants to take things slowly...'

'Ah, but I can see you're in a rush, am I right?'

'Yes, but not for the reasons you think.' Jared grinned. 'I want to live life with her by my side like you and Alice do.'

'Come to dinner on Friday night and bring Rose to meet us,' Toby instructed.

'Thanks, we'll be there,' Jared said as he saw Toby out of the office. He knew for certain they would love Rose as much as he did.

'Tell Sam we send our condolences yet again on his sad loss,' Toby called over his shoulder.

'Will do.'

Jared was about to settle into the big chair to eat his lunch when he heard whistles in the yard. *Now what?* At the doorway, he saw the reason for the commotion. Rose had just walked into the yard. He bolted down the steps and gathered her into his arms. He led her to the office, the sound of their boots lost beneath the explosion of clapping, cheering and more whistles.

'Take no notice of them,' he said as he pulled up a chair for her. 'To what do I owe this honour?'

'I've brought us some lunch so we can eat together.' Rose whipped the tea towel from the basket she'd laid on the desk, oblivious to the paperwork scattered haphazardly.

Unable to stop himself, Jared leaned forward and kissed her cheek tenderly.

Rose smiled and began to unpack the picnic.

'Wait, let me move these first,' Jared said, hurriedly gathering up papers and placing them on a table nearby.

'We have ham, cheese, potted paste, pickled onions and red cabbage, sausages wrapped in bacon – otherwise known as pigs in blankets. Also a ramekin of piccalilli. Apple pie, ginger cake, scones with cream and jam. I expect you to provide the tea.'

Jared laughed loudly as he scanned all the food spread across his desk. Then he hung the kettle on the fire crane and swivelled it over the flames. He felt her eyes on him as he prepared the cups and teapot. Turning about, he said, 'I'm sorry, I'm not keen on ginger cake.'

'No problem,' Rose said as she deftly sliced the cake into thin slices. Going to the door, she yelled, 'Cake here for any who wants it.'

Tim ran up the steps to collect the plate.

'Dad, this is Rose. Rose, Tim Johnson, my father.'

The two shook hands and made small talk while Jared made tea. Then Tim returned to the yard to be ambushed by sorters and grooms, each eager for a slice of cake.

Over their food, Jared explained about the invite to Toby's for dinner.

'I look forward to it. I'll tell the Palace manager I'm unavailable that night.'

Jared slapped his forehead. 'Oh, Rose, I completely forgot!'

'It's all right. It will be nice to have a night off, it'll make a pleasant change.'

'But you won't be earning...'

'It doesn't matter, I'm not destitute yet,' Rose said with a laugh.

'I'll collect you at seven then,' Jared said.

'It's a good excuse to wear my mum's fur coat now the weather is so cold,' Rose stated with a grin.

Tidying away the bits of food left over into the basket, Rose stood to leave.

Jared's heart beat a tattoo in his chest as he took in her fine figure. A sudden thought flashed through his mind of Toby and Alice waiting for years before they could be together. On impulse, he moved to her and dropped to a knee. 'Rose, marry me.'

Rose's eyes widened in shock as she looked down at the man she adored. 'This is... so sudden!'

'I know, but please say you will. Please, Rose, I'll just die if you say no!'

Rose smiled. 'Yes, Jared, I will.'

Jared leapt to his feet and lifted her off hers. He swung her around then stopped to kiss her passionately.

'We'll get you a ring tomorrow. I'll come and take you to the Abyssinian Gold place and you can choose one.' Then, reining in his excitement, Jared said, 'Rose, if at any time you would wish to call off the engagement, please know that you can. I would be heart-broken if you did but I wanted you to know that rather than feel trapped.'

Rose nodded with a smile. 'Thank you, Jared, I appreciate that. Besides, it will probably be a long engagement while we save up enough money for a wedding.'

'True enough,' he agreed, then, as they headed down to the yard, Jared called out, 'Everyone, this is Rose, the lady who has just consented to becoming my wife!'

The couple were instantly surrounded by well-wishers, shaking their hands and congratulating them.

Eventually Rose was able to extricate herself from the press of bodies and left them to their revelry.

'Bloody hell, son, that was a surprise!' Tim said as the others drifted back to work.

'For me too, Dad. I... had to ask when I saw her standing there. If I'd thought about it, I probably would have lost my nerve.'

'I'm so pleased for you.' Tim hugged his boy then returned to his post with the other sorters, a big grin on his face.

Jared went back to the office and sat staring at the empty desktop. He couldn't quite believe what had just happened. He had proposed and she had said yes. Jared Johnson was going to be married! He thumped the desk in joy then winced at the pain lancing through his fingers. *Bloody silly thing to do*, he thought as he rubbed his hands together to dispel the ache.

The smile etching his face would stay in place all day, if not for the rest of his life. He was deliriously happy and nothing could mar that. He couldn't wait to tell the lads when they got back to the yard. He knew they would be glad he had found the courage and taken the leap.

Jared was right in his summation, his friends were delighted for him. Johnny, of course, had something to say. 'Mate, you've only known her but five minutes!'

'True,' Jared said, thinking of him telling Seth the very same thing, 'but I'm certain it was the right thing to do. Besides, if she changes her mind, God forbid, there will be plenty of time to call it off.'

'I'm sure she won't,' Sam put in.

Dan, Paul, Seth and Tom nodded their agreement but were pleased the couple would not be marrying too soon. That way, if it didn't work out for any reason, they could hopefully part as friends.

It was over their evening meal that Seth brought up the subject of him moving out when and if Rose moved in.

'I suppose I could try and rent a room at the Unicorn but how Judith's dad would view that...' Seth said.

'Truth be told, I hadn't even considered that. Everything happened so quickly,' Jared said sheepishly. 'What if Rose wants to stay in her family home? I suppose then it would be me having to move.'

'You can't, this is your home!' Seth exclaimed.

'It's only bricks and mortar, Seth.'

'I suppose, but even so.'

'Look, it's a long way off yet, so let's see what happens when the time comes.'

'Good thinking.'

'Have you noticed how quiet Sam has been since his mum's funeral?' Jared asked.

'I have and it's a worry. I suppose he misses her and he's probably lonely now,' Seth replied.

'We ought to get him out more often,' Jared suggested.

'I agree. Should we talk to the others about it?'

'Yes, let's see what we can come up with when we get our heads together,' Jared said.

The two spent the evening chatting about their girls as usual, extolling their virtues and loving every minute.

The church bell struck seven the following morning and Jared and Seth had to hurry to get to work on time. After he'd opened the yard, Jared set off in a cab to collect Rose. With money in his pocket, he hoped he had enough to cover the cost of the ring she chose.

Rose was excited as she climbed into the cab and it set off for the jewellers. When they arrived, Jared asked the cabbie to wait and he and Rose walked into the massive Abyssinian Gold Jewellery Company. The room was large and filled with light from the large window. There were glass counters with gold and jewels securely locked beneath which glittered and shone. A door led to a back room where it was supposed a large safe would be situated. This would contain the day's takings and any really expensive jewellery. At the end of one of the counter was a high desk which held a till with a large handle on the side; this would be rotated to release the coin drawer. The room was clean but had a sharp odour. Jared guessed the windows had recently been cleaned with newspaper and vinegar.

They were greeted by a thin man with a hawk nose which seemed permanently stuck in the air. 'Good morning, how may I be of assistance?'

'The lady is here to choose an engagement ring,' Jared replied proudly.

'Congratulations. Price range?'

'Erm...' Jared faltered. He didn't have a great deal of money but he didn't want to look cheap in front of Rose.

'I know what I'd like,' Rose said, coming to his rescue. 'One small stone.'

The assistant inclined his head and forced a smile which looked more like a grimace. Clearly he wouldn't be selling any of his best pieces to this fellow. He drew out a tray from beneath the glass counter, having unlocked it with a small key on a chain attached to his waistcoat.

'That one,' Rose said.

The assistant lifted the gold band with a tiny diamond set on filigree shoulders. He passed it to Rose to try on.

'Aw, it's too big,' she said, disappointed it didn't fit straight away.

Pulling out a tapered pole, the assistant took back the ring and slid it on. 'Hmm,' he muttered as he checked the letters on the stick. Putting the ring back in its place, he returned the tray and locked the cabinet.

Jared and Rose exchanged a glance, both thinking the same thing – *he didn't even give us another option!*

'One moment, please.' The man disappeared through a door and a moment later he was back again. 'Would madam care to try this?' He opened the little box and passed it to Rose.

'It's the same ring!' she said, full of excitement.

'Correct, but if I'm not mistaken, and I rarely am, it is in your size.'

Jared took the ring from its resting place and slipped it on her finger.

Rose beamed. 'Perfect!'

Again, Jared saw the sickly smile and the incline of an arrogant head as he gaped at the man. Turning to Rose, he asked, 'Do you like it?'

'Oh, Jared, I love it!'

'Then we'll take it.'

'Would madam be wearing it now?'

'Oh, yes. Jared put it on and I'm never taking it off!' Rose gushed.

'Splendid. I'll just write out your receipt, sir.'

Jared dug in his pocket for his money which was exchanged for the slip of paper and the ring box. 'Thank you,' he said.

'My pleasure, sir. May I suggest you consider us when choosing a wedding band?'

'We will indeed,' Jared said.

As the pair left, the assistant sighed and, holding the money with his fingertips, he put it in the till. The ring they had bought was at the lower end of the price range, but the lady was happy with it. His work there was done, now he just needed a few wealthy customers. 'Ho hum,' he said as he picked up a duster and began to flick it across the glass counter.

Jared took Rose home in the cab, both excitedly looking at the ring on her finger. 'I'll write to my family and let them know,' she said.

Jared gulped; this was something else he hadn't thought about. He really should have done what Seth did and met with Rose's father, but in his haste he'd not even considered it. His stomach roiled at the notion of meeting her family.

Now I know how Seth felt! he thought but said instead, 'Good idea.'

___

27

Clarice had waited impatiently to be on her way to one of the casinos. She had eaten breakfast in the dining room then returned to her room to collect her coat, hat and bag. She had paced the floor, not wanting to arrive at the casino too early. Despite it being open twenty-four hours a day, Clarice didn't want to seem too eager and be talked about by the staff as an inveterate gambler. The lure of the cards, however, was irresistible to her and she knew she had to win big if she wanted to stay at the Midland Hotel. The excitement she felt coursing through her veins had her body on fire and she breathed a sigh of relief when the cab finally stopped.

Paying the cabbie, Clarice knocked on the door and was greeted by the doorman. 'Welcome back, Miss Christian,' he said, allowing her entry.

With a smile and a nod, she walked confidently into the card room. Glancing around as she removed her gloves, Clarice made her choice and stepped smartly to the table. A place was made for her as the gentlemen wished her a good morning.

Clarice removed her coat, which was collected and taken to

the cloakroom by a young woman, then Clarice sat to enjoy a few hands of cards.

By mid-morning, she was well in pocket and with her thanks she rose and, carrying her chips in a small tray designed for that purpose, she meandered into another room where coffee and biscuits were being served. Finding a seat, Clarice let her gaze wander around her. The place was full of well-to-do types, each dressed in beautifully cut suits. Most were older men, probably retired and happy to have found a hobby which took them away from nagging wives. It was in the evenings when the younger revellers were more in evidence.

Laughter and cheers drew her attention as she sipped her coffee. Someone obviously had dropped lucky by the sound of it. Returning the nods of the men as they passed her, Clarice felt like a queen. The respect shown to her was heady and she instinctively knew this was where she was meant to be. She didn't feel at all out of place amongst all these men and because of that she knew she would keep coming back.

Getting to her feet, she placed her empty cup and saucer on the table and strolled away. She investigated another room where games of roulette were being played. In yet another, backgammon was being heavily bet on but it was in the cards room where Clarice felt most comfortable. Returning there, she chose to play whist for a while; a game she excelled at.

By the middle of the afternoon, she had separated the other players from their chips and with tired eyes she decided it was time to call it quits. To groans, she reassured her fellow gamers, 'I will return to give you a chance to win your money back.'

Cashing in her chips and collecting her coat, Clarice left the building. She was ready for a nap before Clifford collected her.

In the cab on the way home, she wondered again if she really needed Clifford. He fed her every night, which saved her spending out on food. He took her to the theatre and beautiful restaurants, but how long would it be before he wanted something in return? Clarice grimaced at the thought of lying with any man, much less Clifford. She didn't want to be bothered with all that nonsense, she just wanted to play cards – and win.

She knew Clifford would tire of her eventually. What man would be content to constantly pay out to have nothing given for his efforts? Part of her wished he would drop her, but the other part knew a good meal ticket when she saw it. If she were honest, she didn't really care either way. Now she was getting known in the gambling dens, she could take care of herself. She was winning far more than the few hands she threw away and that's all she cared about.

Clarice gave a nod; if Clifford came for her then all well and good. If he didn't then she would find a café, eat plenty and get herself to yet another casino.

It was with a yawn that Clarice paid the cabbie and walked into the hotel and on into her room. Removing her coat, she lay on the bed and before she knew it she was fast asleep.

A few hours later, Clarice woke with a jolt. Glancing at the clock on the wall, she was horrified to see she'd slept so long. She had an hour to ready herself before Clifford arrived. Dragging her legs off the bed, she stood and began to undress. Suddenly she dropped back on the bed, feeling woozy. Mentally reprimanding herself for not eating all day yet again, Clarice determined she should start eating lunch, even if it was just a sandwich. Carefully, she stood again and slowly changed her garments. She needed sustenance but for now a drink would have to do. Pouring water from the carafe into the glass on the bedside table, Clarice drank and immediately began to feel better. If she wanted to become rich, she had to take care of herself; she didn't want to be wasting money on doctor's bills.

She noticed her dress felt loose on her and when she checked in the mirror, she saw she had lost a little weight.

With a tut, she shook her head. *This really will not do, Clarice*, she told herself. When she was ready, she descended the stairs to see Clifford waiting for her in the foyer.

'Ah, here she is,' Clifford said.

'Am I late?' Clarice asked, knowing full well he was early.

'It's of no consequence.'

Clarice smiled inwardly; a sign of a spoilt child placing the blame at another's feet. 'Where are we off to tonight?' she asked once they were in the cab.

'Dinner, of course, and then I thought you might like to try out another casino I've found.'

'Marvellous!' Clarice gushed.

Perhaps she would put up with Clifford a little longer after all.

28

On Friday night, Jared collected Rose in a cab and they travelled on to Ivy Lane.

Toby McGuire greeted them at the door and led them through to the living room where Alice sat by the fire.

Rose was introduced and Jared told them all about their exciting trip to the jewellers.

Alice gushed, 'Oh, how lovely,' as she was shown the ring.

Enthusiastic congratulations were given before Toby asked, 'Drink, anyone?'

'Not for me, thank you, I don't drink alcohol,' Rose said.

'What about homemade lemonade?' Alice asked.

'Oh, yes, please.'

'It's in the kitchen, come with me. We can give the men time to chat about work.' The women left Jared and Toby, talking as they went.

'Bloody hell, Jared, it didn't take you long to pop the question!' Toby said once they were out of earshot of the ladies.

'It was spur of the moment, but I'm glad I did.'

'Good on yer, lad. Here, did you ever hear anything more about Clarice Connaught?'

'No, not a thing. I've not seen her either since that day at the music hall.'

'Ah, yes, I remember you telling me about that.'

Jared went on, 'If what her father told me about her is true, then I consider myself lucky to be out of it.'

'To be sure. Rose is the one for you, 'tis plain on both of your faces,' Toby said as he passed Jared a glass of beer.

'We'll have to make sure we have the time to get to know each other properly before we wed,' Jared said.

Toby nodded as he sat, drink in hand. 'How are the lads getting on?'

'Fine, although I'm worried about Sam.' Toby frowned and Jared went on, 'I think he might be terribly lonely. He seems quiet and a bit withdrawn.'

'It's no wonder. He lived with his ma for all of his life and now she's gone he's bound to feel lonesome.'

'I suggested we get him out more in the evenings,' Jared confided.

'It would certainly help, although with both you and Seth having sweethearts, it might be awkward.'

'Rose sings at the Gaiety Palace most evenings and Judith works the bar at the Unicorn with her dad, so we could manage if we work it right.'

'I think it would do him good and you never know, it might be he meets a girl of his own,' Toby said.

'Right, you two, dinner's ready so get your arses into the dining room,' Alice called.

The two men exchanged a grin when Toby said, 'She has a mouth that would put a navvy to shame, so she has.'

Jared chuckled as he followed the big Irishman through to

where Alice was serving up a beef roast with all the trimmings. Toby poured wine for the three of them; Rose content with her lemonade.

'Dig in, we don't stand on ceremony here,' Alice urged.

'This looks and smells delicious, Alice,' Jared said, his mouth watering at the tantalising aromas.

'Ar, well, eat your fill, lad.'

Between bites, Jared passed on information about Seth and Judith and the other tatters.

'Seth and Judith are head over heels for each other, I think they could be married before too long,' Jared said.

'How is Sam getting along?' Alice enquired.

'He's doing all right. I sometimes catch him staring into space for a moment, clearly he's thinking about his mum. It will take some time for him to get over her loss, I think.'

'It's a hard thing to lose your mother,' Alice added.

'I can't imagine how I'd feel if I lost mine,' Rose said.

'And how are the lads getting on with the rounds?' Toby asked.

'Fine, but I think we could do with maybe thinking about extending out to other towns. I'll have to investigate whether Wednesbury, Darlaston and Walsall have any tatting going on. If not, I see a lot of business coming our way. Of course, I wouldn't want to step on any toes if there were thriving tatters in the vicinity.'

'Very thoughtful, lad. Get on to it is what I say.' Toby grinned as he glanced around the table.

'I'm not sure how the boys will take to going further afield, though,' Jared confessed.

'They'll do it if their wages were upped by a few pennies,' Toby suggested.

'Fair enough.' Jared knew the extra money would come in

useful for all of them, especially for Seth, who was saving for his wedding.

'I'm so glad Seth moved in with you, Jared, 'cos it was the making of him, especially after what Ned did to him. I remember the state of him when Toby brought him here,' Alice said.

'Ah, but you nursed him back to good health, Alice,' Jared replied, 'and you, Mr McGuire, found his long-lost mum.'

'You and I together, Jared. Had you not visited that neighbour in the first place, we may never have found Mrs Watkins,' Toby responded.

Rose listened as she ate; she was learning more about her intended as the conversation proceeded, and she was glad to know she'd made the right decision by accepting his proposal.

'Jared tells me you sing down at the Palace, Rose,' Toby said.

'I do, but not every night. I love singing and so when my family moved to Wednesbury I decided to stay on here.'

'Do you get to see 'em, cocker?' Alice asked.

'Yes, every few months I go over on the train, it makes for a nice day out.'

'I expect they'll be excited to hear your news about the engagement,' Alice went on.

'I've written to tell them, so I should hear back soon but yes, I think they'll be happy for us.'

'I'm guessing you've not set a date for the wedding yet?' Alice asked.

'No, I'm not sure when—' Rose began.

'I know we said we would wait until we knew each other better but I have to admit the sooner the better for me,' Jared interrupted.

Alice's laughter filled the room then she eyed her spouse. 'See, Toby McGuire, that's how it should be done.'

'I asked you in the end, didn't I?' he said, feigning hurt.

'Ar, yer did. I'm just glad these two have years of married life together ahead of them.'

Jared and Rose grinned at each other across the table then Rose said, 'We could have a Christmas wedding.'

'Oh, that would be lovely,' Alice said. 'Snow and pretty lights would be so romantic.'

'I agree,' Toby said, 'a winter wonderland wedding.'

'Ooh, hark at him getting all poetic,' Alice quipped and everyone laughed loudly. 'Besides, it will give you a good twelve months to learn all you need to know about each other.'

'I was actually thinking of this Christmas,' Rose said sheepishly.

Jared choked on his food and Toby banged his back. 'That's what, three weeks away?'

'Well, if you don't want to,' Rose pouted but with a wink at Alice.

'Yes! I do, but will we have enough time to organise it?' Jared blustered. This had taken him by surprise to say the least; it seemed they were both prone to impetuosity.

'Ah, but it's simple. You go and see the vicar and sort out the banns to be read out in church. Rose goes and buys a new frock and Bob's your uncle, Fanny's your aunt – all sorted,' Toby said, spreading his hands wide.

'Ain't that just like a bloody man – buy a new frock indeed!' Alice exclaimed. 'First of all, it's a wedding gown and it'll probably have to be made, or altered if it's off the peg. Then there's invitations, flowers and reception to see to.'

Jared and Toby shared a look which said, *Why all that fuss?*

'Look here, Rose, with your family away in Wednesbury, I'd be glad to help as long as they don't think I'm stepping on any toes,' Alice said as she grabbed Rose's hand.

'Thank you, Alice, I know my mum would appreciate that.'

'I suggest after you've seen the vicar the pair of you get over there and talk to Rose's family,' Alice suggested.

'I agree, you can meet my dad at last,' Rose said, squeezing Alice's hand. Alice returned the gesture and they grinned.

'Oh, shit!' Jared pushed his empty plate away as everyone burst out laughing.

29

Over the next few days, Rose had gone to see her parents in Wednesbury and arranged for them to meet Jared. In the meantime, Jared had set out to see the vicar of St Bartholomew's. His excitement grew as he walked swiftly to the church and arriving at the churchyard he was surprised to see a horse and cart there. He had decided to make a short visit to Sam's mother's grave to pay his respects and as he approached, he saw Sam standing at the graveside.

'Sam?' Going to his friend, he spotted the tears. 'Aw, mate,' Jared said as he wrapped an arm across Sam's shoulder.

'Sorry, Jared, I know I should be working but...' Sam managed on a sob.

'I understand.'

'What are you doing here?' Sam asked.

'I've come to see the vicar about a wedding,' Jared replied.

Sam nodded. 'That's marvellous, Jared, good for you. I promise I'll get back to work, I just needed...'

'Have a moment with your mum first. Oh, and by the way,

we're having a night out tonight so get your glad rags on. I'll come round your house to pick you up at seven o'clock.'

'Thanks, Jared, I could do with that.'

Jared left Sam and walked to the church. Nothing had actually been arranged for that evening, it was a sudden thought as he'd watched his pal grieving. However, he knew it wouldn't take much to persuade the lads, and they would all be in agreement after he told them what he'd witnessed here.

An hour later, when Jared exited the church, Sam and his cart were gone. Jared sprinted over to Rose's house to tell her they were to be wed on 20 December at one o'clock. As Toby had said, that gave them plenty of time to get organised.

Jared had told the lads he was closing the yard at lunchtime today so to be sure to be back on time. He had somewhere to be later that afternoon; he was meeting Rose's family and he was as nervous as hell. What if they didn't like him and tried to stop the wedding taking place? Jared's stomach clenched at the thought and he silently prayed all would go well. He had to impress Bill and Joan Whitman as well as Rose's brother, Joshua. Over their many conversations, Jared had learned of his in-laws-to-be and that Bill was a manager at a nail-making company. Joshua was still at school but would be leaving soon to find work. From all reports, Rose's was an easy-going family and Jared hoped that would prove true.

On his way back to the yard, he popped in to see Toby and Alice to give them the good news of the time and date of the wedding. Trudging back to work, he wished his own mum and sister were here to see him wed. Entering the yard, he went straight to his father and whispered, 'One o'clock, 20 December.'

Tim frowned.

'I'm getting married.'

Tim grabbed his boy in a bear hug. 'Congratulations, lad, I'm so pleased for you.'

'What's going on?' one of the sorters asked.

'You are all invited to my wedding on 20 December at one o'clock at St Bart's,' Jared yelled.

Whistles and clapping filled the air and one by one the Cavenor brothers, the sorters and grooms came to shake his hand. When all the noise died down, Jared told the brothers about seeing Sam mourning at the graveside. 'I thought we could take him out somewhere tonight, but I don't know where. Do you have any suggestions?'

Bobby and Dicky shared a quick glance and Bobby replied, 'We know just the place. Can we come as well?'

'The more the merrier,' Jared replied.

'Bring your wallet 'cos you'll need it,' Dicky said.

Jared frowned. He had no idea what the Cavenors had planned but he didn't question them. It would be a nice surprise for them all.

Jared spent the rest of the morning planning new routes for the following week and was astonished at how quickly the time had passed. The carts came in one by one and Jared explained the idea for the evening and why it had been planned.

Once the horses were seen to, Jared locked up the yard. He had just enough time to wash and change his clothes before collecting Rose for their train journey to Wednesbury.

'Scary, in't it?' Seth asked as they reached home. 'Meeting her folks, I mean.' Jared nodded. 'They'll love you so don't worry.'

'I hope so.'

Jared rushed around washing in cold water, donning his decent clothes and refusing lunch. His stomach really couldn't cope with food. Saying a farewell, he hurried out to find a cab.

Rose was ready and waiting when he arrived at her house in

Fox Street. It stood opposite a public house and was noisy at night when the punters turned out but Rose was usually singing at the Palace so was not overly bothered by it. They drove on to New Street station and were amazed by the crowds pushing their way through the entrance. There were hawkers standing around shouting prices for their wares, a baker with bread panniers on the side of his horse. A fellow was selling wooden toys he whittled and painted, soldiers and horses. A woman carried a basket full of posies of herbs, doing her best to attract customers. A young boy was shouting, 'Papers, come and get your newspapers here!'

Jared stood in line to purchase the tickets before they strode onto the platform. It was packed and they were pushed and shoved as people milled around, impatiently awaiting the train's arrival. At last, the rumble heralded the iron beast was on its way, and as its wheels screeched to a halt, it puffed out a great cloud of steam. Ladies coughed into lace handkerchiefs as the doors were flung open and people spilled out to cause mayhem on the platform. It was a free-for-all as folks jostled to be the first to board in order to procure a seat.

Grabbing Rose's hand, he said, 'Stay close to me.' He jumped up onto the steps of the train and dragged Rose behind him.

Jared used his elbows to protect Rose from the bustling crowds then he barged down the carriage and quickly snapped up two spaces on the wooden bench. The doors slammed shut, a whistle blew and the train began to puff as if out of breath. As the brakes were released, the carriage jolted and a moment later it began to slowly move forward. They were on their way.

In no time at all, they were pulling into Wednesbury station and grinding to a stop. Here the platform was not nearly so busy and Jared and Rose alighted without any fuss. Leaving the station at a more leisurely pace, they walked along the tramway into Victoria Street, which was lined on both sides with houses covered in grime. An industrial town, Wednesbury was constantly beneath a pall of smoke from household chimneys which burned in summer and winter alike. Passers-by nodded a greeting and children ran around in bare feet and ragged clothes, clearly not feeling the cold. A chimney sweep cursed loudly as his bicycle hit a rut in the road and he veered off dangerously, only just keeping his balance. The pair walked on towards the Holyhead Road and coming to a neat little terraced house, Rose said, 'Here we are.' It was a two up, two down squashed between others just like it but in contrast its windows sparkled like gems in the weak sunshine. The brickwork looked as though it was cleaned often of the soot which floated in the air night and day. The front doorstep had a high shine, having been polished with Cardinal Polish. Even the front door knocker held a gleam from a thorough working over with Brasso.

Jared gulped. It was now or never. With a nod, he followed her along a ginnel leading to the backs of the row of buildings.

'Ready?' she asked.

'Yes,' Jared said but shook his head.

Rose laughed and then walked in through the back door. 'It's only me,' she called out, knowing her voice would be recognised. Jared frowned.

Anyone could be saying that, it could be a burglar, but then if it were would they announce their presence? Jared took a deep breath as Joan Whitman came rushing into the kitchen, arms outstretched to embrace her daughter. 'Hello, love.'

'Hello, Mum, this is Jared.' Rose stepped aside and pushed Jared forward.

'I'm pleased to meet you, Mrs Whitman,' he said with a croak. His nerves jangled at the woman who eyed him suspiciously.

Joan's eyes slipped briefly to her daughter's belly then they locked eyes. Rose shook her head and Joan breathed a sigh of relief.

'Welcome, Jared, come on in and I'll make tea. Rose, your brother is through there, he just got home from school. Your dad won't be long, he's finishing early today as we're going to the music hall later.'

Rose and Jared went through to the living room and Jared immediately liked the place. A fire crackled in the hearth and the chairs and settee looked comfortable.

'Hello, Joshua, this is Jared.'

The boy stood to shake hands. 'Nice to meet you, Jared. Hello, our Rosie,' he said, giving his sister a hug.

Joan brought in a tray of tea and instantly the talk began around the wedding. Rose had told her mum about their getting married on her previous visit, and now she spoke of Alice's offer of help and Joan beamed with pleasure that the couple had such good friends.

'Have you set a date yet, love?' Joan asked excitedly.

'The vicar said he could squeeze us in on 20 December at one o'clock. I know that doesn't give us much time to prepare but—'

'Are you happy, sweetheart?' Joan asked, her voice full of concern.

'Oh, yes, Mum, I am very happy!'

Joshua rolled his eyes and, addressing Jared, said, 'You want to come and see my pigeons?'

Jared nodded and they went into the yard to a small pigeon loft where the birds cooed and billed. Despite the cage being clean, there was a sharp tang of ammonia which hit Jared's nostrils and made his eyes water. Joshua, however, didn't seem to notice and Jared thought that perhaps he was used to it. Tiny feathers floated down as the fan-tailed birds fluttered their wings, obviously eager to be let loose to grace the sky with their beautiful flight.

'Do you race them?' Jared asked as he tried to breathe through his mouth.

'Not yet. I'm training them to home first, then I might.'

'They'll do well,' a deep voice said.

'Hello, Dad, this is Jared, our Rosie's intended.'

Bill Whitman shook Jared's hand and Jared winced inwardly at the iron grip.

'Sir, I know it's customary to speak with you before... I'm sorry but it was all rather spur of the moment before I lost my courage.'

'Do you love my daughter, Jared?'

'Yes, sir, I do, with all my heart.'

'Then I will just say this; you hurt her in any way, shape or form and I will hunt you down and no one will ever find your body.'

Again, Jared gulped, then he croaked, 'Sounds fair to me.'

Joshua howled with laughter as they all went indoors for tea.

30

'Joshua, get up in the loft and fetch the box just to the side of the hatch, please,' his mum requested and Joshua disappeared. After some banging and clattering, he returned with said box.

Joan opened it up and drew out her own wedding dress, holding it up for all to see. The champagne silk was overlaid with the finest Nottingham lace and tiny covered buttons ran the length at the back. Passing it to Rose, she then lifted out a silver tiara with three silk roses attached to the top.

'If you take it to a dressmaker, she'll be able to take it apart and make it into something just for you. It will save you some money.'

'Oh, Mum! I wouldn't dream of it. I'd much rather wear it as it is, if it fits,' Rose gushed.

'Let's go upstairs and try it then.' Joan's eyes brimmed with tears.

'Mum, what about Jared seeing it before the wedding, won't that bring bad luck?' Rose asked.

'Superstitious nonsense, love. From what I remember the old 'uns saying, this came about because of arranged marriages. The bride's family would hide her away until the day of the wedding then place a veil over her face in case the groom didn't like the look of her. By the time they got wed, it was too late! I'm sure you've heard the old saying as well: *Something old, something new, something borrowed, something blue,* but I'll bet you didn't know the last line was *and a silver sixpence in her shoe.*'

'No, I didn't, but if you expect me to walk around all day with a coin in my shoe, you're sadly mistaken.' Rose laughed and hugged her mother. Joan's tears fell like rain as she hugged her daughter back.

'I'll make a fresh brew,' Bill said, wiping away a tear of his own.

'And I'll lay the table, otherwise we won't get fed!' Joshua added.

'What can I do?' Jared asked.

'Slice the ham for some sandwiches 'cos it looks like a cold tea today,' Bill answered with a grin.

Upstairs, Rose stripped down to her chemise and Joan helped her into the dress. With the tiara on her head, Rose spun around. 'I can't believe how well it fits, Mum.'

Joan smiled. 'I was your size when I married your dad, not that I'm much different now.'

'Thank you.' Rose hugged her mother and they each shed a few tears.

Rose took off the tiara and placed it beside the box, then once the buttons were undone, she slipped out of the dress which Joan folded and laid in the box, placing the tiara on top while Rose dressed.

Fully clothed again, Rose sat on the bed next to her mother.

'Rose love, I know you said that all this is a bit sudden and I want to know if you're positive you're doing the right thing. Are you sure?'

'I am, Mum, in fact I'm certain. I love Jared with all my heart and soul and we plan to grow old together.'

'Does he feel the same way?' Joan probed.

'Yes, Mum, you don't have to worry about us. We're going to finish up like you and Dad. You two will love each other until the end and Jared and I will be the same, I promise.'

'That's all I wanted to hear. Come on, let's see the look on your dad's face when I tell him we all need new outfits!'

Rose giggled as she carried the box downstairs. Joan was right, Bill's face was a picture as he counted the cost in his mind of two new suits and a dress and hat.

Joan, Bill, Jared and Rose sat squashed around an old scrubbed table in the kitchen to enjoy a tea of cheese, ham, fresh bread and butter, tongue, pickles and cold sausages. Joshua took his plate to eat in the living room where he had more space.

Bill had built a tiny pantry in one corner of the kitchen and a cupboard on the wall held crockery and glassware. Cutlery lived in a drawer in the table. The window had been replaced for a bigger one and let in lots of light, despite the overcast weather, and pretty curtains hung at the sides. The wooden chairs were upright and uncomfortable but were small enough to fit around the table.

'You will give me away, won't you, Dad?' Rose asked once they had finished eating.

'It would be my honour, sweetheart,' Bill answered.

'We'll be there on the day, but if your friend, Alice, can help with flowers and such it would put my mind at rest,' Joan put in.

'We'll sort it all out, don't worry,' Jared said reassuringly, before saying they should be on their way. He explained about Sam and why he and the boys were taking him out for the evening. Rose added that she was booked to sing at the Palace too.

So with hugs and handshakes the happy couple left, the box containing the dress tucked firmly under Rose's arm.

Boarding the train, Rose said, 'See, it wasn't that bad after all.'

'You have a smashing family, Rose, and I'm glad to be marrying into it.'

* * *

Later that evening, the Cavenors, Paul, Dan, Sam, Johnny, Tom, Seth and Jared walked across town to a building down a dark street.

Bobby knocked and they were let inside by the doorman, who greeted them all like long-lost brothers.

There were gasps of surprise as everyone took in their surroundings. 'How did you know about this place?' Jared asked.

Dicky tapped the side of his nose and jiggled his eyebrows.

'We knew you liked playing cards,' Bobby said as they sauntered around the small casino. Gas lamps cast a yellow glow over the gaming tables and a shabby carpet collected mud and water from countless shoes that passed over it. The wallpaper had seen better days but the shadows hid most of the damage done to it over the years. Old and battered chairs sat around the tables for those wishing to sit rather than stand.

'Now I understand your remark about bringing my wallet,' Jared said with a grin.

'You change your money for chips over there,' Bobby instructed as he pointed to a booth where a woman with heavy make-up stood waiting.

'You can have a drink or there's coffee if you prefer,' Dicky added, nodding to another other room reached via an archway.

'Right, let me at it!' Johnny said, rubbing his hands together.

'Hang on a minute,' Bobby said, grabbing the young man by the collar. 'Set yourself a limit and don't go over it. I've known men lose everything in these places. Play for fun and then walk away.'

'We will,' Dan said.

'This is serious,' Dicky emphasised, 'you may win a bit or lose a bit, just don't go overboard.'

'Thanks, we'll be careful,' Sam said before they began to wander around.

Each exchanged some money for chips and headed off to their table of choice. They took full advantage of the baccarat, whist and poker games and each had a thoroughly good time.

Around ten o'clock, the Cavenors rounded up the gang, saying it was time to go home.

'What time does this place close?' Johnny asked as they waited in line to give back the chips and retrieve any money owed.

'It doesn't, that's why you have to be strict with yourself and know when to quit,' Bobby answered.

Giving their thanks and goodnights to the doorman, the group walked away from the club. Dan said he was down by one shilling and threepence, Paul had lost a tanner, Tom had lost a shilling, Seth and Jared had broken even. Johnny had lost the lot; Sam was the only winner, he was up by half a crown.

'You lucky bugger!' Johnny exclaimed.

Sam grinned as the others congratulated him. 'I like that place,' he said.

'Ar, while you're winning, you do. Then when you start to lose, you'll bet everything you've got just to win again. Gambling's like a drug, it gets a hold of you and won't let go until you're destitute and livin' on the streets.' Bobby let his words sink in before he went on. 'Men have lost their houses, their families, all they have to those places. I even heard of a bloke betting his missus.'

'Did he win?' Paul asked drily.

'No. He had to give her up to honour the bet.'

'Bloody hell!' Dan muttered.

'She had her own back, though, d'aint she, bro?' Dicky said.

Bobby nodded. 'Yeah, she went back home the next day and stabbed her husband to death.'

'No!' Tom blurted out.

'It's true, every word. That's why we said set a limit and stick to it,' Dicky said.

'Well, I'd like to go again sometime,' Sam put in, 'but not often. Just as a treat now and then.'

'Sensible,' Bobby commented.

Thanking the Cavenors, they parted ways and went home, the tale of the woman and her knife looming large in their minds.

31

_____

Clarice had searched the town earlier for a dress shop and bought herself some new dresses. Much as it galled her to spend her money, she felt it was time to update her wardrobe lest Clifford wonder why she wore the same clothes time after time. She chose garments that looked expensive but cost very little, that way she could purchase more as and when needed. She also chose a couple of scarves to tie around her neck cravat style and a hat with netting that covered her eyes; she thought it very chic.

That evening, Clifford and Clarice were in yet another casino. She was amazed there were so many in Birmingham. How come she'd never heard of them before now? Probably because she hadn't been anywhere but the marketplace before she ran away from home. It was of no consequence, she was well acquainted with them now.

Just the sight of a large building with a casino sign over the door made Clarice's anticipation rise as they approached. This was not a dingy place in a dark back street; this was on show for all the world to see.

Inside, the rooms were brightly lit with huge gasoliers and

lamps on the walls. There were carpets on the floors with green baize-topped tables everywhere. Roulette games were in full swing and the men at the bar stood three deep.

Clarice noticed she was one of very few women other than the waitresses. The young girls carried silver trays with boxes of Havana cigars on them or empty glasses being taken to be refilled, the little piles of chips denoting their gratuities.

The rooms were abuzz with chatter, laughter and losers' groans and Clarice was immediately caught up in the fervour of it all. She couldn't wait to get sat down with cards in her hand.

'I meant to ask you, m'dear, did your pater's cheque arrive?' Clifford asked as they wandered through to another room.

Clarice was taken by surprise at the question and had to think clearly. 'No, unfortunately not as yet.'

'Ah, that's jolly bad luck.'

'Indeed, in fact, if it were not for the small amounts I've won recently, I really don't know what I would do.'

'Of course, I could always extend a helping hand...' Clarice was all ears. 'In the form of a loan, naturally. I would not wish to offend you by stomping on your independence, you understand.'

Oh, I understand, all right! Clarice thought but said instead. 'Thank you, but there is no need. I will manage. Ah, a table for me there, I think.' With that, Clarice walked on, leaving Clifford looking a little bewildered by her sharp tone.

Throughout the evening, Clarice slipped from one table to another, gradually accumulating a nice pile of chips. By the time they left, she was decidedly better off.

On the way home, she thought again of Clifford's suggestion of a loan. *I suppose that's why some folk are rich, they hang on to their money – they don't give it away.*

Nevertheless, Clarice couldn't help but be annoyed and she

was no good at disguising it. Sitting straight-backed in the cab, she left Clifford in no doubt that she was irritated with him.

Clifford, for his part, had no idea what he'd done to rile her so he sat pondering the situation.

Arriving at the hotel, Clarice climbed from the carriage, and with a curt goodnight she left Clifford standing in the dark, wondering at her swift mood swings.

In her room, Clarice threw her bag on the bed and paced the floor. *Bloody men! Trust me to pick a miser with only half a brain!* She had thought he would have realised her predicament and given her some money to tide her over. But no, the thick-headed dolt had done no such thing. Chivalry and good manners were one thing, but this was quite another.

Sitting on the edge of her bed, Clarice took out and counted her winnings. Her anger dissipated as she eyed the notes in her hands.

You can stick your money up yer arse, Clifford St John, I'm doing very nicely on my own, thank you very much!

* * *

The next morning was greeted by a crisp frost covering the land in a thin layer of white which crackled and crunched beneath the boots of people going about their daily business. Women had thick woollen shawls wrapped around their shoulders and tied beneath their breasts; another draped over their heads and secured at the nape of their necks. Hefty skirts over cotton petticoats which hid woollen stockinged legs and feet shoved into well-worn boots. Few had the luxury of a winter coat so layer upon layer of clothing had to do to beat off the cold.

Men fared no better as vests, shirts and jumpers were covered by jackets buttoned up tight. Mufflers were wound around throats and flat caps were pulled down low over tired eyes. Those lucky enough had moleskin trousers, and hand-knitted socks covered cold feet inside old boots.

Plumes of steam flowed from open mouths, the air too cold to draw in through the nostrils which would sting and burn. Everywhere folk hurried through the streets, intent on getting their business concluded quickly so they could return home to a roaring fire.

Winter had arrived in Birmingham and everyone knew it would be months before they would have respite from the biting cold and, no doubt, the fall of snow which would hamper their travels.

The coal jagger was delighted to be rushed off his feet as he delivered sacks of coal to customers from his horse-drawn cart.

The knocker-upper was having a hard time getting people out of their beds in the morning as she fired pea after pea from her shooter at people's bedroom windows.

Horses pulling carts struggled to gain purchase on the slippery cobblestones and traffic slowed to walking pace. Chimneys belched out grey smoke which hung heavy in the air, covering the land like a shroud. Cabbies sat waiting for fares, having dressed warmly and wrapped themselves in thick blankets. The men on the bread line stood close to makeshift braziers, burning anything they could get their hands on.

Anyone living on the streets began to fear for their lives for it was certain a good number of them would perish before winter's end. Grave-diggers cursed as they fought against iron-hard earth with picks and shovels, the whole thing taking twice the normal length of time. Doctors and hospitals ensured their dispensaries were well stocked before the usual cold weather illnesses struck. The city of Birmingham was in the throes of preparing for a long hard winter.

Jared and Seth shivered, despite wearing their overcoats, as they crossed the heath to the yard.

Once indoors, the Cavenors lit the braziers and Jared called for the blankets to be brought out from the large cupboard in the corner. The sorters hung them from a low crossbeam to air out.

'If it starts to freeze, get yourselves back here. The business won't fail for missing a day's trade, but it will if you all go down with pneumonia,' Jared said as they all gathered for a hot brew before setting out. 'The blankets will help once they've aired out a bit.'

Within half an hour, the carts left the yard and Jared's worry began. The last thing he needed was for anyone to fall sick. He recalled how, in the past, McGuire had told them the same thing and now as manager the responsibility lay with him. He knew he would only relax when all of his friends were back, suffering no ills from the drastic change Mother Nature had imposed on them.

32

Over the next week, the weather warmed up a little but the clouds had still brought snow. However, that didn't stop Clarice from visiting the casinos during the daytime. She spent the morning in one and the afternoon in another. She alternated between the many she now knew existed and, slowly but surely, she was becoming a wealthy woman.

Clifford still arrived at the same time every night to collect her and Clarice continued to treat him like dirt. Why the man put up with her, she would never know, but her taking advantage of him was ceaseless. He bought her dinner, took her to the theatre or the music hall on occasions, and paid for the cabs. Clarice didn't spend a penny except when gambling, and winning more than losing, she considered that a good deal.

As she sat sipping coffee and watching the players, Clarice smiled inwardly. Her pretence of being a lady fairly high-born was standing her in good stead. No one was aware of her true background and that's how it would stay as far as she was concerned.

Handing her empty cup and saucer to a waitress, Clarice stood and walked over to a table where she was welcomed warmly. She had time for a few more hands before going home. The excitement flowed through her as the cards were dealt. Gambling was her drug of choice and she knew she could never give it up. She was also aware it could make or break a person but she played on regardless. Her lifestyle would either see her living in a mansion or, God forbid, on the streets.

By early afternoon, Clarice left the casino and headed home. She decided she would have afternoon tea at the hotel then take a nap.

Over tea, sandwiches and cake in the hotel dining room, Clarice nodded to people coming and going all dressed in fine clothes; they were wealthy and clearly they thought her the same.

Retiring to her room, Clarice wondered what Clifford had in mind for entertainment that evening. Lying on her bed, listening to the crackling of the fire, she hoped it would not be a boring play.

After a short but refreshing sleep, Clarice rose to wash and change. She realised she could do with buying some more new clothes but she was loath to spend her money as yet. One could never know how the cards would play out and Clarice intended to hold on to what she had, for now, anyway.

At seven on the dot, Clifford arrived and informed her that after dinner they would be attending a soiree at his friend's house. 'I can't wait to show you off. I feel so very lucky, Clara, and I know everyone will be envious when I walk in with you on my arm.'

Clarice saw this as a golden opportunity to integrate with rich and powerful people and was already looking forward to it.

They ate at a fine restaurant and Clarice again relied on her escort to suggest a meal. She finally decided on a chicken dinner and ate with gusto. Eventually the time came to depart and travel to the soiree.

'Who is your friend, Clifford?' Clarice asked once in the cab and on the move.

'Anthony Purcell, oh, but you met him that night outside the theatre.'

'Yes, I recall,' Clarice said with a forced smile. She had not taken to the man at all, though he had given her no reason to dislike him. She just felt like he could see through her façade to the real person beneath and that scared her. No one must ever discover who she was and she prayed her new persona would stand up to the test.

The cab turned off the dimly lit quiet street and rolled up the long winding drive which was lined with trees. It came to a halt outside a massive house with light shining from its many windows. There were three steps which led to the front door, which was flanked by Greco Roman columns. The knocker was fashioned in a huge lion's head. Stepping from the carriage, Clifford banged on the door.

It was opened by a butler and the couple were invited in before being relieved of their outdoor clothes by a maid. Then they were shown into a huge room. People were milling about chatting and Clarice was stunned at the opulence of the place. Large gasoliers lit up the room and chairs were set out in rows. Heavy damask curtains hung at the windows and on one wall a massive fireplace held a fire big enough to burn a tree. A baby grand piano took up the whole of one corner of the room.

'Ah, there you are,' Anthony called out as he crossed the room towards them.

'Hello, you remember Clara Christian, I'm sure.'

'I do. Welcome to my home, Miss Christian.'

'Thank you, Mr Purcell. It certainly is beautiful.'

'Do help yourselves to champagne,' Anthony said as he waved over a waitress with a tray full of glasses. 'I must greet my other guests, please excuse me.'

Clarice took a flute of champagne and watched Anthony hurry to welcome in more people.

A huge man and his small wife arrived and Anthony shook their hands. He said something and the big man let out a loud belly laugh. Anthony spoke again and Clarice heard the wife say, 'I don't bloody think so, you bugger!'

Common as muck! Clarice thought as she and Clifford took a seat.

A moment later, the big man and his wife were sitting next to them.

'Toby, how very nice to see you. Alice, you are lovelier than ever,' Clifford gushed. 'May I present Miss Clara Christian. Clara, this is Toby McGuire and his wife, Alice.'

'How do?' Alice said.

Toby nodded his greeting, a slight frown creasing his forehead. He was sure he knew this young woman from somewhere but he couldn't quite place her.

'How is business?' Clifford asked the big Irishman.

'Ticking over nicely, so it is. I have a manager in place now, Jared Johnson, so I can enjoy my semi-retirement.' Toby saw Clara's eyes dart to Clifford and back at the mention of Jared's name.

'It's all right for some,' Clifford guffawed, 'others of us have to keep working, eh, m'dear?' He turned his eyes to Clarice who smiled sweetly.

'Indeed, Clifford.' Then to Toby she added, ''E works so hard.' Her beau had missed her slip into the local vernacular but the McGuires had picked up on it.

Alice threw a glance Toby's way, asking *is she who I think she is?* With a raised eyebrow, Toby had answered with *I'm thinking so.* 'Miss Christian, is it?' Toby asked quietly. 'Strange, but I could have sworn your name was Clarice Connaught.' Seeing the colour drain from her face, both Toby and Alice knew he was correct in his thinking.

'How very odd, Clara was mistaken once before for someone called Clarice, do you remember, dear?'

'Yes, Clifford, I do now you mention it,' Clarice said, feeling decidedly sick. How did this big Irishman know her?

'You must have a twin out there somewhere, what?' Clifford gave a snort.

Both Clarice and Alice cringed but Toby simply stared. So this was what Clarice was up to. Just as Jared had said, she was out with a toff. She didn't know him but Toby knew her. He'd seen her often in the market and heard her name called. After all, how many women with the name of Clarice lived in Birmingham?

Clarice was obviously uncomfortable beneath Toby's gaze and excused herself to visit the powder room.

Alice was on her feet like a shot. 'I'll come with you, I could do with a piddle before the fun starts.'

Clarice swept from the room with Alice on her heels.

'It's this way, cocker,' Alice called out as Clarice turned the wrong way. 'I've been 'ere before as you might have guessed.'

Clarice nodded as they entered a beautifully laid out bathroom.

'Now then, madam, why don't you tell me what's going on?' Alice rounded on Clarice, her tone threatening.

'I have no idea what you mean,' Clarice tried to bluff it out.

'I think you do. You snubbed young Jared Johnson when he

spoke to you that night. You hurt him, Clarice, he rather liked you up until then.'

Clarice closed her eyes and exhaled. She had been found out, but the question now was – how could she get herself out of this calamity?

33

'Look, you don't understand!' Clarice said in a harsh whisper.

'I'm listening,' Alice responded.

'I just wanted to better myself. I had to get away 'cos my father...'

'I know of him and he ain't what you purport him to be. It turns out that everything you told Jared was a lie!' Alice said vehemently.

'Please don't tell Clifford who I really am.' Clarice knew she had to beg if she was to try to keep up the charade she had woven for herself. 'He'll drop me like a hot potato if he finds out.'

'And rightly so, if you ask me.' Alice curled her lip. She really didn't like this girl very much at all.

'Alice, please!'

'You should go and see your father, he's been worried sick over you.'

'I will, but I'm begging you not to say a word to Clifford.' Clarice had agreed to Alice's request but had no intention of keeping to it.

'Right, well, I'll say only this and then I'll let the matter rest. I won't mention a word to Clifford because I can see he's besotted with you. He is also Toby's friend so if you hurt Clifford, you can be sure he'll know the truth about you 'cos I'll be singing like a canary. Also, should you see Jared again, don't you dare snub him. He's engaged to be married so he's no longer interested in you and I, for one, am happy about that.'

'Thank you, Alice,' Clarice said, breathing a sigh of relief.

'Remember what I said 'cos if needs be, my Toby can find you.' With that, Alice turned Clarice around and pushed her towards the door.

Once back in the company of their men, Alice said, 'Toby, this lady is not who we thought she was.' She gave her husband a surreptitious raise of her eyebrows that Toby immediately picked up on and understood its meaning.

'Ah, now, I am to be apologising for my mistake, Miss Christian, so I am.'

Clarice inclined her head.

'Well, at least that's that settled, now we can enjoy the evening,' Clifford put in.

Clarice grabbed another glass of champagne from a passing waitress's tray and took a gulp, then forced a smile to hide her discomfort.

Anthony Purcell clapped his hands to gain everyone's attention. 'Lords, ladies and gentlemen, please take your seats and join me in welcoming the maestro, Senor Pablo Hernandez.'

The last posterior landed on a luxurious cushion just before a well-built man in coat tails strode into the room followed by a young fellow carrying sheet music who took his place at the piano and placed the papers on the stand.

Acknowledging the applause with a bow, Pablo nodded to the pianist, who tinkled the ivories with an introduction. Then

Pablo began to sing, his beautiful tenor voice sailing effortlessly out across his audience.

Clarice remained uncomfortable throughout and couldn't wait to get out of the place. She felt sure that nosy Alice was watching her but each time she glanced in the woman's direction, Alice had her eyes on the singer.

After each song, shouts of 'Bravo!' echoed around the room and the applause was loud; Clarice clapped along with everyone else although to her ear the singing was just a racket. She had no idea why these people would enjoy such a thing.

Eventually, after the last song, the impresario began to introduce Pablo to his guests, the young pianist having left to apparently attend another recital across town.

When they came to Clarice, Pablo kissed the back of her hand and Clarice smiled warmly at the gesture. This is definitely how she should be spending her time; living the high life.

Anthony drew Pablo away and Clarice's eyes sought out the meddling Alice. She saw her deep in conversation with her husband, were they talking about her? As if to confirm her fears, Alice looked in her direction and wiggled her eyebrows. Clarice gave a barely perceptible nod and turned away to accept yet another glass of champagne.

'Steady on, old girl, we don't want you trying to outmatch the tenor on our way home!' Clifford guffawed at his own wit.

Clarice glared at him, downed her drink then said, 'I'm tired, Clifford.'

'Ah, right. I'll just say goodnight to Anthony and we'll be away.'

Clarice sighed heavily. She was tired – of this bumbling idiot. Now he'd dropped her right in the shit by bringing her here because Alice bloody McGuire had discovered her ploy. Did this mean she'd be looking over her shoulder all the time, wondering if people she didn't know would recognise her? She shook off the thought as Clifford re-joined her.

Their cabbie, who had waited patiently wrapped in a blanket, drew the carriage to the entrance for the couple to board.

'Midland Hotel,' Clifford called up to the driver.

But only for a few minutes, Clarice thought, because when you've gone, I'm off to the casino!

As they travelled, Clifford extolled the virtues of the tenor but Clarice merely mumbled her agreement. Her mind was on the card tables and she couldn't wait to get there.

'How strange, though,' Clifford said, dragging her attention back.

'Sorry?'

'That the McGuires mistook you for someone else as did that young man at the Gaiety Palace.'

'Oh, yes.'

'I take it you straightened it all out in the powder room.'

'We did indeed,' Clarice said.

'Jolly good,' Clifford said before they fell into a companiable silence.

Arriving at the hotel, Clifford helped her alight and with a kiss to her cheek said, 'I'll see you tomorrow.'

'Tomorrow.' Clarice watched the cab roll away and, waving to another waiting nearby, she said, 'Monty's, please.'

'Yes, ma'am,' the cabbie replied as he waited for her to climb aboard.

Bloody soiree! Bloody Alice McGuire!

34

At the yard, Jared sidled up to his father. 'Dad, would you be my best man?'

Tim's face beamed. 'Of course, it would be my honour. I thought you'd ask one of your pals.'

Jared shook his head. 'I'd like you to do it 'cos we're family.'

'That we are, son. Just over a week to go, is everything ready?'

'Rose has her gown, she's ordering some flowers and I've arranged the church.'

'What about a reception?' Tim asked.

'We can't really afford it, Dad, so a drink in the Unicorn will have to do.'

Tim nodded. 'That will be fine, I'm sure.'

It was then that Toby's booming laughter rang out as he greeted the Cavenors; he had arrived for his weekly visit.

'Is this how you spend your time, standing around gossiping like old women?' Toby asked, striding over to them, a big grin on his face.

'Jared's asked me to be his best man. We've just been

discussing how it will be back to the pub for a drink after the ceremony,' Tim explained.

'It will be no such thing!' Toby boomed, drawing all eyes to him. 'You can have your reception over in Ivy Lane, God knows the place is big enough.'

'Mr McGuire, that's very kind of you but we can't afford a reception,' Jared said quietly.

'Let it be our wedding present to you both then. Alice will be in her element putting on a good spread. I'll tell her when I get back.'

'Tell her?' Jared asked with a raised eyebrow.

'All right, *ask* her, but you know Alice, she'll love the idea.' Toby grabbed Jared in a bear hug. 'Come, we have work to do!'

'Thanks, Mr McGuire,' Jared said once they were ensconced in the office. 'Rose will be so pleased.'

'Rose is a lovely girl, Jared, and she's just right for you, not like that other one you had your eye on. We saw her last night, you know.' Jared shook his head with a questioning frown. 'Only Clarice Connaught, so it was!'

Toby explained everything that had taken place at the soiree, and when he'd finished, Jared said, 'It's sad that she has to pretend she's someone she's not. I guessed that was the case when she claimed not to know me. I feel sorry for her because I can't help but wonder if it will all come to a disastrous end for her.'

'That's her look out, so it is. You just need to concentrate on getting wed.'

After checking the books, Toby left to inform Alice that she would be hosting a wedding reception – with a very big *please* to accompany the news.

Striding back to Ivy Lane, Toby stopped occasionally to exchange words with people who shouted a greeting. A woman with a toddler on her hip asked after Alice and Toby assured her his wife was in good health. A young man shouted across the road, asking if Toby had any jobs going; his reply was he would let the fellow know as soon as a position came up as there was a possibility the business could be expanding.

Reaching home, he called out to his wife, 'I'm home.'

'About bloody time an' all,' Alice retorted but with a cheeky grin.

Over tea in the kitchen, Toby related to Alice what he'd told Jared about having the reception at Ivy Lane.

'You did the right thing,' she said.

'What, no ranting and raving?' Toby asked, feigning surprise.

'You know me better than that, you bugger!' Alice exclaimed.

Toby laughed. 'You'd best get some shopping done, then.'

'Ar, I'll get a list drawn up.' Alice moved to fetch a pencil and paper and began muttering to herself as she wrote. 'Beef, pork and stuffing, cheeses, fruit...'

'I'll make a brew,' Toby said and smiled when Alice just nodded.

'Beer, wine, oh, and I'll have to polish the silverware and check we have enough glasses. Napkins, plates...'

Toby left her to it, putting the kettle to boil.

That evening, Jared and Rose went to dinner early as Rose was not singing at the Palace.

'We'll have to decide where we're going to live once we're wed,' Jared said.

'I'd like to come to you,' Rose answered, 'that way I could rent out my family home.'

'How would your parents feel about that?'

'I don't think they'd mind but I could go over and ask them just to be sure. I can make a day of it and spend some time with them.'

'What about Seth? How can I tell him he has to move out?'

Rose sighed. 'I didn't think about that. Well, you'll just have to move in with me.'

'I... Rose, don't take this the wrong way but...'

'I know, you want to stay where you are.'

Jared nodded.

Rose blew out her cheeks at the dilemma facing them both. 'We'll sort it out somehow. Let's have our dinner then go to the Unicorn and have a chat with Seth and Judith.'

Jared instantly felt a little better at that idea. Maybe they could work it out between them.

* * *

In her room at the Midland Hotel, Clarice was counting her money. She had won big at Monty's the night before so she secreted most of her winnings in a bag in the wardrobe. Checking her look in the mirror, she nodded, picked up her gloves and bag and walked down the stairs. Now she was ready and waiting for Clifford to collect her.

I hope there's no more bloody soirees! she thought as she stood in the hotel foyer.

'Hello, darling, my, you look lovely,' Clifford said as he came in out of the cold. 'I have a table booked for dinner, so let us be away.'

Clarice nodded as he held open the door for her. She wondered about what he had planned for after dinner.

Once seated in the fine restaurant, Clarice hit upon an idea to solve her problem of being unable to read. As the waiter brought the menus, Clarice waved it away. 'I'm in the mood for beef – well done.'

The waiter nodded and turned to Clifford.

'Good idea. I'll have mine rare.' Clarice inwardly winced. She couldn't eat anything a good vet could get back on its feet. She sipped her wine and glanced around. She didn't particularly want to talk to Clifford, she just wanted to eat then go to a casino as soon as she could.

'Penny for your thoughts?' Clifford asked as he gazed at her across the table.

The question took her by surprise and Clarice took another sip to give her time to come up with a lie.

'Nothing much, sweetheart,' was the best she could do.

'Where would you like to go after dinner?'

'Well...' Clarice began. Now was her chance to say where her heart lay – the gaming tables.

'I know, you want to play cards again,' Clifford said.

'Do you mind awfully?' Clarice asked, laying her hand on his.

'Of course not, darling, anything for you.' Clifford melted like ice in springtime.

'Thank you, my love.' Clarice removed her hand and picked up her glass once more. With that settled, she was now intent on enjoying her dinner, making sure not to look at Clifford's meat oozing blood everywhere.

Over at the Unicorn, Jared tried his best to explain to Seth about what he and Rose had discussed earlier about their living arrangements after the wedding.

'Rose wants to move in with me, but that means—' Jared began.

'I have to move out,' Seth finished for him. 'It's all right, Jared, we have discussed this before and we both knew it would come. I can soon find somewhere to lay my head.'

'I'm sorry, mate, I've racked my brains to find a good outcome for us all but I can't.'

Judith was on her break and instantly found the solution.

'If Rose moves in with Jared, I could rent Rose's house!'

'Could you afford it?' Seth asked. 'And what would your dad say about it?'

'Dad would be fine, but I have to admit it would be a struggle moneywise,' Judith admitted.

Jared and Rose exchanged a look. They were thinking the same thing – maybe Judith was trying to nudge Seth in the direction of marriage. Seth and Jared had already discussed this and

Jared knew his friend was going to ask Mr Kingston for Judith's hand. It was the 'when' that had Jared foxed.

'Look, let's ask Dad what he thinks,' Judith said and yelled for her father to join them at their table near the bar.

'Pokey, look after the bar a minute,' Joe yelled as he made towards his daughter.

Judith told him about their discussion and Joe nodded. 'It would make sense to do it that way provided everyone was in agreement, including your family, Rose.'

'You don't mind Judith moving out of here then?' Seth asked.

'No, she's old enough now to be making her own way in life, but I'd like for her to remain working here.' Turning to Judith, he asked, 'What do you say, sweetheart?'

'I'd taken that as a given,' she answered.

'Right, but I have to say – two wages going into the house would be better than one.' Kingston winked at Seth and moved back to his place behind the bar.

'What the hell was all that about?' Seth asked.

Jared stood and dragged Seth outside towards the privy at the back of the pub.

'What?'

'Seth, you imbecile, that was Mr Kingston's way of telling you he approved of you and Judith.'

'I know he does, he allows us to walk out.'

Jared sighed. 'He was saying if you and Judith chose to wed, he was okay with it!'

Suddenly the penny dropped and Seth nodded slowly, his mouth hanging open. 'So I wouldn't have to ask him then?'

Jared grinned. 'No, you just have to ask Judith – and properly, the whole flowers and one knee thing. You could do it better than me!'

'Bugger that!' Seth turned and marched away.

Jared closed his eyes. Had he spoiled things for Seth with Judith by suggesting what he had? Spinning around, he followed his friend back indoors and there he found Seth on one knee before Judith, who was nodding.

Applause rang out as the couple embraced, then cheers sounded when Kingston yelled, 'Drinks are on the house, my girl is getting wed!'

'Blimey! He's as impulsive as you,' Rose said with a laugh.

'He's been talking about proposing but he just needed the courage to ask her dad.'

Seth and Judith were congratulated by all as they raised their glasses in a toast.

When time was called, Jared and Seth walked Rose home then returned to their own house. 'You'd best see the vicar soon,' Jared said.

'Yeah, I'll have to rent a room somewhere for a few weeks after you're married.'

'Why not ask Mr Kingston if you can stay at the Unicorn? Tell him you don't want to waste your money on a boarding house,' Jared suggested.

'Good idea. I'll speak to him tomorrow night.'

'The lads will be pleased for you.'

Seth nodded. 'Oh, I'll have to get a wedding ring an' all.'

'Bloody hell, so will I!' Jared exclaimed. 'Another visit to the Abyssinian Gold Jewellery Company it is then.'

The two friends grinned before spontaneously dancing a little jig around the kitchen.

* * *

Once again, Clarice was at the gaming table and she was losing badly. She couldn't understand it, she rarely lost unless it was on purpose. She moved to another table but the bad luck followed her.

'Looks like Lady Luck has forsaken you this evening, my sweet,' Clifford said over her shoulder.

Close your gob before I slap it! Clarice thought as she watched her chips being raked in by a fellow player. She *had* to win them back! Nodding to the dealer, Clarice checked her cards – another rubbish hand. She knew she should quit after this round but she so desperately needed just one more win.

By ten o'clock, Clarice was out of the money she had brought with her. Giving her congratulations to the others, she stood to leave.

On the way home, Clarice's thoughts went over every game she had played. How could she have come out so badly?

Clifford was rambling on but she didn't hear a word he said. Then suddenly a thought struck. Were those men she had played with known as 'card sharps'? Another thought followed hot on the heels of the last. Could the casino have brought them in because they suspected her of cheating?

'Clifford, please be quiet, I have the most horrendous headache,' she snapped.

'Sorry, m'dear.'

After a quick perfunctory kiss goodnight, Clarice rushed to her room. What the bloody hell was going on? Sitting in the chair by the fire, Clarice racked her brains for an answer, but as the flames began to die, she was no closer to finding one.

The following morning, Clarice took a little from her savings and headed out for one of the other casinos. She needed to know if her luck had truly deserted her or whether her suspicions were correct. If she won, it was all to the good. If she lost, then that would certainly suggest the casinos were on to her. The fact that she was *not* cheating would not be taken into consideration. She would be banned with no further ado.

This can't be happening! What shall I do if I can't play cards any more?

Again, Clarice lost every game she played and went home thoroughly baffled.

Little did she know she would be in for another surprise later that evening.

36

Clifford picked Clarice up at the usual time but he was cagey as they travelled to have dinner. It was after they had ordered that he said, 'You don't seem very happy, m'dear.'

'I'm fine.'

'Is it because you didn't win at the tables last night?'

'I don't understand it, Clifford,' Clarice said.

'Clara, I think it's time you came clean with me.'

Clarice frowned. 'About what?'

'You told me you didn't know how to play and yet you fleeced everyone – regularly. It is my contention that you lied to me.'

Clarice clamped her teeth together before saying, 'I'm sorry, Clifford, but it was only a little fib.' Clarice knew the game was up as far as the cards were concerned.

'Clara, a lie is an untruth whether it be large or small. I'm disappointed in you, I can't deny it.'

'Clifford, I just wanted to play!' she said in a harsh whisper.

'You *needed* to play, Clara. You have an addiction, don't you realise that?'

'I do not! I merely enjoy—'

'They're on to you, m'dear. The casinos have sussed you out.'

Oh, my God, so I was right! The words slammed into her mind.

'I suspect if you try to go again you will be refused admittance,' Clifford said flatly.

'No matter, there are other places,' Clarice said defiantly.

Clifford shook his head. 'Clearly you don't realise what this means.'

'Tell me then!'

'Your name will be blackened and word will be passed to every casino in town. You will be branded a cheat and banned from the clubs.'

'But I'm not a cheat!' Clarice rounded on him.

'It doesn't matter whether you are or you are not. The house doesn't care, all they see is that you were taking money from them and they won't put up with that.'

Clarice stared at him, knowing he was right. Just then, their order arrived but Clarice had lost her appetite. She pushed the food around on the plate before shoving the plate away.

'Not hungry?' Clifford asked as he tucked into his own meal.

'Not any more,' Clarice mumbled.

'I'm sorry, m'dear, but I thought it best you should know.'

Clarice nodded. She had been playing this morning but evidently word hadn't reached them at that time, but they would be aware by now. She wanted to bang on their doors and scream her innocence. She wanted to prove she wasn't what they thought but she knew it would be impossible even if they let her in. They would just say she had been counting cards, in other words – cheating!

'Is there anything else you have lied to me about, Clara?' Clifford asked, breaking her train of thought.

Clarice shook her head miserably.

'Then can you explain to me why, on two different occasions, two different people have called you Clarice?'

'Mistaken identity,' she answered, a coldness settling in her stomach.

'Really? I'm sorry but I don't believe that. You see, my friend, Anthony, has deduced you are not who you say you are. It appears that you really are Clarice Connaught who once lived in Erskine Street.'

Clarice's mouth fell open. How the hell had he found out? Had Alice McGuire told after she had said she wouldn't?

'I see by your reaction that I am correct. Tut, tut, *Clarice*.' Clifford dabbed his mouth with a napkin then sipped his wine.

'I'm not sitting here listening to this drivel!' Clarice said as she got to her feet. Willing him to ask her to stay, she stared at him.

'Goodbye, Clarice, it was nice while it lasted,' he said. Sadness filled his eyes as he watched her stamp away.

A sense of loss overcame him and he felt tears prick his eyes. Pushing his plate away, he gulped his wine. He would never have known had Anthony not quizzed Toby McGuire about Clara Christian. Alice may have promised not to say a word, as she told Anthony, but Toby hadn't and he sang like a bird. It had been at lunch that very day that Anthony had revealed the truth to his friend.

Clifford sighed. Part of him wished he hadn't found out, but part was glad he had. Clarice Connaught was taking him for a fool but despite all that – he still loved her.

Leaving the restaurant, Clarice had hurried home to the hotel and now sat before the fire, her temper just barely in check. If it did turn out that Alice had talked... *I'll bloody kill her!*

Tapping her foot on the floor, Clarice wondered what would happen now. She couldn't gamble and that galled her most of all.

She dreaded the thought of trying to nab another suitor, especially one as gullible as Clifford. The money she had left wouldn't last long and then she'd have to leave the hotel. To go where? She could go back to her father, but she guessed he'd tell her to sling her hook.

An image of Jared rose in her mind unbidden. Would he help her? Shaking her head, she recalled what Alice had said. *You hurt him, Clarice, he rather liked you up until then... he's engaged to be married...* No, she'd find no aid from that quarter. Clarice knew she was, yet again, on her own.

In her haste to leave, Clarice had not noticed Anthony Purcell sitting in the bar. He had watched them carefully whilst Clarice and Clifford were in the restaurant and when he saw her jump up and rush away, he joined his friend at the table.

'You were right, Anthony,' Clifford said miserably.

'I'm sorry, Clifford, I was hoping I wasn't – for your sake.'

'She never admitted to any of it, in fact she denied it to the last, but it was evident that she was indeed Clarice Connaught. What made you suspicious in the first instance?'

'From the first time we met her, I guessed. Every now and then I caught a very slight change in her accent as she slipped into the local vernacular. She was good, Clifford, but not quite good enough.'

'I have to confess I didn't pick up on it.'

'Perhaps your feelings towards her blinded you to it.'

Pouring Anthony a glass of wine, Clifford said, 'Tell me everything.'

37

'Do you recall telling me Clara was staying at the Midland Hotel?'

'Yes, we had lunch a couple of days after Clara – *Clarice* – and I began to see each other.'

Anthony nodded. 'Well, I had a quiet word with the night clerk there one evening after attending the theatre. It was a gut instinct, so I followed it through. He informed me there was no Clara Christian staying at the hotel. He also told me about a woman being dropped off in the early hours who stepped into the foyer. When her beau left, she rushed outside and disappeared into the night. This seemed further proof that *Clara* was staying elsewhere.'

'Oh, hell, this just gets better and better!' Clifford said woefully.

'This then led me to wondering how our mystery lady spent her daylight hours.'

Clifford ordered another bottle of wine as Anthony went on.

'I remembered you saying how lucky she'd been at the casino. No beginner at cards is so fortunate as to win so often, so

I took a trip there myself. It seems Clara had been visiting the tables during the daytime too.'

Clifford shook his head, hardly able to believe what he was hearing.

'When I enquired about her, the management were very surprised to hear she purported to be only just learning. They said she had been winning often and at times quite large sums.'

'I did wonder where her money was coming from as she said her father's cheque had still not come through from America,' Clifford proffered.

'Ah, well, therein lies another story. Toby McGuire confided that Clarice's father has a job at the brick works right here in Birmingham.'

'Hellfire and damnation!' Clifford boomed.

'It appears Clarice Connaught is lazy, refused to go out to work; she spread foul rumours about her father being a drunken bully, then one day she upped and left.'

'I can't believe it of her, Anthony.'

'It's true, my friend, every word of it. When she and Alice McGuire retired to the powder room at my soiree, Clarice was forced to admit who she was. She begged Alice not to breathe a word to you and Alice agreed and has stood by that. She did, however, tell her husband, who in turn, spoke to me.'

'Christ, can it get any worse?' Clifford was feeling more wretched by the minute.

'That young man who approached her outside the Gaiety Palace...?' Clifford nodded. 'She did know him. He's Toby's manager at the yard and she'd even been out with him for afternoon tea!'

Clifford stared into his wine glass. 'I've been such a fool,' he said quietly.

'You weren't to know, you were in love.'

'The pity of it all is – I still am.'

'The question is, was that love reciprocated?' Anthony asked gently. He could see his friend was suffering agonies over all that he'd heard, but felt it would be better to get it all out in the open in one go.

Clifford shook his head. 'I suspect not. I'm of the belief now that she was using me to get to where she wanted to be.'

'I'm afraid I have to concur.'

'What will I do without her?' Clifford asked mournfully.

'You will pick yourself up and go on with your life.'

'I was thinking of proposing to her, you know.'

'I'm bloody glad you didn't! My dear fellow, how would you have felt had she refused you?'

Clifford's reply was a deep sigh.

'Precisely. Even had you wed, how long would it have lasted?'

'Knowing what I do now, probably not much over six months would be my guess.'

'Clifford, I'm sorry it's turned out this way and that I was the one who had to tell you, but I really couldn't watch her take you for a mug any longer.'

'I know and I appreciate it, Anthony, I really do, it's just that I was praying it was all a big mistake.' Then, as a thought struck, he asked, 'Were the casinos really on to her?'

'When I spoke with the management at Monty's, we came up with a plan to try and catch her out. They brought in a team of men, card counters, who they use quite often for this kind of work. I'm damned if I know how they work it, but they beat Clarice at every hand.'

'Was she cheating?'

'It seems not; apparently she's just a bloody good card player but she was bleeding the house dry. They consulted with the other gaming houses and she was going from one to the next and

so on, earning herself a substantial amount at each. So they
agreed a ban was in order.'

'It's probably for the best. Clara only ever wanted to go
gambling, I think she may have an addiction.'

'Believe me, Clifford, you are better off out of it.'

Clifford nodded but he didn't really think so because no
matter how hard he tried, he couldn't get the woman he knew as
Clara Christian out of his mind.

'Come on, let's take brandy in the bar,' Anthony suggested.

'Now that's the best thing I've heard all night,' Clifford said,
pushing to his feet.

38

That night, large snowflakes fell in silent abundance, covering the landscape like a white fluffy blanket. When Jared drew back the curtains in the early morning, he gasped in surprise. In the snow he saw the tracks of a bird, likely looking for food, and he made a mental note to put out the bacon fat before they went to work.

Dressing quickly, he went downstairs to rekindle the range. He shivered as he set the kettle to boil. He shoved the frying pan containing eggs and bacon onto the hotplate and cut some bread to be fried in the liquor.

As he stared out of the window, he wondered if Rose would manage to get to Wednesbury today. She was going to see her folks to ask about renting their house to Seth and Judith once they were married. He didn't know if the trains would be running due to the weather.

The other thing, of course, would be how the horses would cope. Snow wasn't so much of a problem but the frozen roads beneath could be treacherous as he knew from years past. He'd just have to see how things went when he got to the yard.

'Bloody hell, it's cold!' Seth said as he came into the kitchen.

'Have you seen that lot out there?' Jared nodded towards the window as he turned the bacon in the pan.

'Oh, crikey, where did all that come from?' Seth muttered as he warmed his hands by the range.

'I'm thinking it might be a day at the yard helping to sort today,' Jared said.

'That would suit me fine,' Seth answered as he shivered again.

'It might be wise to wear extra socks and pull out our wellingtons. We can take our boots with us and change when we get there.'

'I'll fetch them.' Seth headed for the cupboard under the stairs and shook out the wellingtons to ensure there weren't any spiders which might have taken up residence there.

With hot tea and a good breakfast inside them, they began to warm up but neither wanted to leave the cosy kitchen.

Jared threw the bacon scraps out for the birds then they donned overcoats, scarves, caps, wellingtons and gloves. Boot laces tied together, boots hung around their necks and snap tins tucked under their arms, they set off. Shoving their gloved hands in their pockets, they trudged through the virgin snow, leaving a furrow in their wake. Their breath plumed from their open mouths as they went and the cold bit their noses and ears, turning them red. The only sound to be heard was the dull crunch beneath each footstep. Even the birds were quiet, clearly opting to stay in warm nests a while longer.

Rose had also trudged through the snow and was pleased at being told by a porter that the trains were still running. 'A bit of snow won't stop our drivers,' he said proudly.

Rose was looking forward to seeing her family again and if the weather took a turn for the worse, she could always stay overnight. The Palace and Jared knew where she was going so neither would worry unduly if she wasn't back that evening.

Over at the Midland Hotel, Clarice cursed the weather; she had plans and now the snowfall had buggered them up. She knew she would have to wait a day or so for the thaw and then she could go about her business unhindered.

Counting her money for the third time in an hour, Clarice knew she had to find a way to bring in some more.

Bloody casinos, who did they think they were to ban somebody from their tables?

Clarice glanced down at her hands and realised they were shaking. It wasn't because they were cold, so was it anger or was she suffering anxiety from being unable to gamble?

Building up the fire, Clarice sat in the chair, staring at the dancing flames, the mesmerising effect making her feel drowsy. She soon fell asleep and dreamed of winning big in all the casinos she had frequented, much to the chagrin of the owners.

Rose spent the day with her mum, planning and chatting about the upcoming wedding. She had asked about renting the house to Seth and was pleased when it was agreed. Then, with hugs and kisses, she trudged along to catch the late afternoon train back to Birmingham. Calling in at the Palace to let them know she was home, she was rather relieved when she was told she would not be needed that night. The manager was of the opinion that few customers would brave the dropping temperature to attend anyway. Rose left and made her way to her house, trying to avoid the filthy slush of the streets; foot and cart traffic having turned the pristine white snow into a brown sludge. Glad to be indoors once more, Rose settled to making herself a meal and enjoying the heat of the kitchen.

Over at the yard, Jared had instructed the grooms and sorters to go home early. Despite the large braziers, they were cold to the bone. The Cavenors too were happy enough with their boss's decision and it didn't take long for the yard to be locked up securely.

Jared was following McGuire's lead of days gone by when he too sent them home, not expecting them to work in such bad conditions. The business had not suffered then and it wouldn't now. People could always find something to exchange for a penny or two. Tomorrow was another day and Jared would wait and see what Mother Nature would bestow upon them before making any decisions.

39

After a couple of days cooped up in her hotel room, Clarice had begun pacing like a tiger.

Now that the snow had finally melted away, she could put her plan into action. As darkness fell, she wrapped up warmly and set out. She walked briskly in order to beat off the cold but also so that she could reach her destination quickly. She had considered taking a cab but with what she had decided to do, she thought it might prove unwise. Tongues wagged and if a cabbie was asked about her, he might squeal. She did not want to be seen or recognised by anyone, and the dark night and shadows would hide her from prying eyes.

Coming at last to the building, Clarice slipped stealthily to the rear where she crouched, silently watching and listening for any signs of life. Satisfied that she was alone, she crept to the door and turned the knob. It swung inwards with only the merest of squeaks. One small gas lamp on the wall was all that illuminated the room. Stepping inside, she glanced around. The kitchen – excellent. Close to the range was a dumb waiter. This could turn out better than she could ever have imagined.

She whipped a tea cloth from the rail above the range and looked around again. There were curtains at the windows which were pulled closed.

Opening the door to the range using the cloth, she pulled out the rolled-up newspaper from her pocket. Shoving the end into the flames, it caught quickly. Holding it beneath the curtains, she smiled wickedly as they began to burn and give off smoke.

Closing the range door again, she laid the cloth on the hotplate and dropped her overlarge taper onto it. Smoke plumed and she blew on it to ensure the cloth ignited.

For a moment only, she watched the smoke disappear, sucked into the dumb waiter like a chimney. A burning curtain fell onto a wooden chair and another onto the table pushed beneath the window.

Clarice turned and fled the room, happy that it was now well alight. Walking briskly away from the building, she smiled into the darkness. A little way down the street, she stopped in a patch of deep shadow and watched as people fought to get out. Shouting and screaming could be heard as men and women poured out of the front door in fear of losing their lives.

With an evil chuckle, Clarice walked away. Monty's was being razed to the ground and Clarice didn't give a damn. That would teach them to ban her!

She knew that by the time the fire truck had been summoned and had arrived, it would be too late to save the casino. After an investigation, the conclusion would be that the cloth on the rail had fallen down and caught alight.

Clarice had seen for herself the people scrambling out of the doors and if anyone had been left inside as the fire raged, it was their tough luck. It served them right as far as she was concerned. Besides, it would be the owner who would be held responsible. There was no way it could be traced back to her.

Once more in her room, Clarice danced a little jig. One down; now to draw up plans of how to dispose of the others. Sitting by the fire in her hearth, Clarice grinned. Monty's would be in ruins by now, the firemen fighting a losing battle.

Moving her mind on to the next one, Clarice suddenly had a thought. If all the casinos burned, would someone put two and two together and come up with the name of Clara Christian? Then by process of further investigation perhaps tie her to the Midland Hotel?

It was possible; the constabulary were wily fellows. Just to be sure, Clarice decided it was time to move. She'd find a cheap boarding house on the outskirts of the city where no one would think to search for her. Then she could proceed with her plans of arson: every casino she had played in would burn to the ground, and after each one she would change lodgings. If she kept on the move, they would never catch her. Once her vindictive streak had been satisfied, Clarice would board a train to another big city where she could start again.

There were gambling houses everywhere, surely? It would not take her long to find out, but until then Clarice had to eke out her money. With what she considered to be so little left, she had to work quickly. She also guessed the next *job* might not prove nearly so easy. She would have to think this through carefully.

Monty's would be seen as an accident; clumsy work on someone's part, so the next would have to be in the same vein, at least it must look accidental. If she couldn't manage that then bugger it, deliberate arson it would be!

Across town, crowds had gathered, hampering the fire truck reaching the inferno. Loud explosions shook the road and people screamed and yelled, ducking to escape the flying debris as the windows blew out, but still they didn't move away. Water was being pumped onto the conflagration from the barrels on the truck which were emptied in no time. The firemen shook their heads, knowing they could do no more. They boarded and returned to their station, leaving the building to burn itself out. They had done all they could to ensure the fire would not spread; fortunately the building was well away from its neighbours.

The folks watching the blaze slowly dispersed as they saw the flames beginning to die down, their discussions on how the fire had started still hot on their lips. Some thought it was a shame, others were happy the casino had gone, although they prayed no one was inside when it went up. Almost all wondered if it would be rebuilt and how much money it would cost to do it.

Back in her room, Clarice was having much the same thoughts. It didn't matter to her for she had sought and exacted her revenge on those she felt had treated her so cruelly.

Now, how to bring the next casino to its knees?

* * *

The next day, the newspapers were full of the incident and tongues wagged on every street corner, in shops and around the market.

Jared had read about the terrible accident and asked his staff to be extra vigilant with sorting the rags and ensuring the braziers were kept at a safe distance. Having heard the gossip, everyone agreed with his request.

'Tomorrow is the day, son,' Tim Johnson said as he stood next to Jared. 'You excited?'

'Yes, but I'm scared stiff. What if I'm left standing at the altar and Rose doesn't show?'

'She will. Every groom has pre-wedding nerves. You'll be all right, you'll see.'

'He's right, lad,' Toby's voice boomed out as he entered the yard.

'Mr McGuire, I didn't expect to see you here today,' Jared replied.

'Ah, but I had to get out of the house. Alice says I was getting under her feet. She's enough food to feed the five thousand, so she has.'

'It's good of you both and we appreciate it.'

'My good lady wife is in her element, Jared, every time I went to the kitchen to make a drink she yelled, "Toby McGuire, don't you dare touch that food else I'll chop your bloody fingers off!" Christ, I ain't master in my own home any more!'

'You never were if you'd be honest with yourself,' Jared quipped.

'Ain't that the truth?' Toby said then, his laughter resonating around the yard, made everyone else smile. 'Do you be having everything you need for tomorrow?'

'I think so. I collected Rose's wedding ring this morning and my suit is clean and ready.'

'Well now, Tim, your lad is getting married, how're you feeling?'

'I'm as proud as punch,' Tim replied.

Toby nodded. 'Next will come the patter of tiny feet,' he said with a cheeky grin.

'Now hold your horses there, Mr McGuire, I ain't even wed yet!' Jared said with a horrified look on his face.

Laughter echoed around as sorters and grooms enjoyed the banter.

A while later, Toby left, saying it was time for him to go home and face running the gauntlet once more. Alice wielding a rolling pin was a daunting prospect but being a big, tough Irishman, he would do his best to cope.

That evening, Jared locked up, knowing it would be the last time for a few days. He gave the keys to the Cavenors, who promised to look after the place while he was gone. Jared and Rose would spend a little time settling her into her new home.

Seth had taken the few things he owned and moved into a room at the Unicorn the previous day. Once Rose had moved to Jared's, Seth would go to Rose's house until the day he married Judith, which was in a month's time. It was like playing pass-the-parcel but with houses.

Sitting before the fire alone, Jared's mind overflowed with thoughts. Tomorrow night he would be sharing his house and his bed with Rose. Nerves fluttered in his belly as he prayed he could live up to being a husband in the biblical sense. It would be a squash in his single bed but once Rose was here, she could order a double and be there to see it installed. The single could then be shoved beside Seth's in his old room.

His mind conjured up pictures of his mother and sister and he wished, yet again, that they could be here; they would have loved Rose. Suddenly the enormity of it all overwhelmed him and he felt warm tears trickle down his cheeks. Sadness for his lost family merged with happiness at marrying Rose and Jared gave in to his feelings and wept. Only when he was cried out did he head to bed, exhaustion making his body heavy. At least now he hoped he would sleep well.

CHARLES TERRYSON

40

Tim arrived at Jared's house around eleven o'clock to ensure everything was in order. He was taking his role as best man very seriously.

Jared had taken a bath and was having a cup of tea in the kitchen, dressed only in clean underwear and wrapped in a blanket.

'Tea in the pot, Dad, freshly brewed,' Jared said.

'Ta, lad.' Tim helped himself. 'You all set?'

'I think so. Oh, there's a flower there for your buttonhole. Rose dropped them off yesterday, she left them by the back door.' Jared watched as Tim secured the flower into place then said, 'You look great, Dad, thanks for doing this.'

'Like I would have turned you down!' Tim answered with a grin. 'Son, I'm so proud of you.'

'Thanks, Dad.' Tears welled in Jared's eyes as his father threw his arms around the blanket-covered young man.

After a moment, Tim took a seat, wiping away his own tears.

'Dad, can I ask you... about tonight,' Jared said, embarrassment written all over his face.

'Of course, lad. Look, follow your instincts but remember to be gentle with her. Rose will be – still intact, so be prepared for her pain at the beginning. There may be blood but that's natural and it's nothing to be afraid of. There could be tears as well because the emotions will run high in both of you but if you are considerate, it will not spoil the pleasure, nor will it frighten her off.'

'Bloody hell, it's like planning an invasion!' Jared gasped.

Tim laughed loudly. 'Savour it like you would a good brandy because it will only get better with time.' Jared blew out his cheeks. 'Come on, get dressed for it's time to be off.'

They arrived at St Bartholomew's in plenty of time and welcomed Joan and Joshua, whom Jared introduced to his father. The lads came all looking smart, as did Toby and Alice. The Cavenors were next and took the pew at the back of the church almost as though they were still on guard duty. Lots of Rose's friends from the Palace were also in attendance, dressed in bright colours as if they were primed and ready to tread the boards. Thespians in large feathered hats strutted around waving silver-topped canes, shouting, 'Hello, dahling!' Dancing girls giggled in a huddle when Johnny and Dan cast glances their way but it was Sam who led the ladies to their seats. Seth and Judith walked up the path arm in arm. The organ played gently in the background as everyone chatted quietly while they waited for Rose to arrive.

'Oh, sweetheart, you look a picture,' Bill Whitman said as his daughter descended the stairs dressed in her mother's wedding gown.

Rose smiled then flew into her dad's arms. She felt his body heave as he tried desperately to control his feelings, but his tears flowed nonetheless.

Then, pulling himself together, he said, 'There's still time, love, if you want to change your mind.'

'No, Dad, I want to do this with every fibre of my being.'

Holding her at arm's length, he said, 'Come on then, let's get you wed.'

The vicar took his place, nodding to Jared as the wedding march was played and Rose and her father stepped slowly down the aisle.

Jared gasped as his eyes took in her beauty. It was like looking at an angel; the winter sunshine through the window casting a myriad of colours around her. Her smile was honest and true as she nodded to the guests. She was almost undone as she saw her mother sobbing, but she faced her betrothed and her smile returned.

The service began and throughout Jared never took his eyes off his beloved Rose. It all seemed to pass in a blur for him and before he knew it, he was kissing his bride to loud applause.

Outside, the guests pelted them with rice before they climbed into the pony and trap the lads had hired between them. Ribbons and flowers decorated it all over and the horse wore a plume of white feathers.

Toby had sorted out a line of cabs to take everyone back to Ivy Lane to enjoy a good spread and to raise a toast to the happy couple before drinking themselves silly.

As the trap jogged along, Jared said, 'I love you with all my heart, Mrs Johnson.'

'And I, you, Mr Johnson – husband of mine,' Rose returned.

They kissed then banged noses as the trap went over a raised cobblestone. Laughing together, they waved to bystanders who shouted their good wishes.

Life was about to change for Jared and he welcomed it with open arms.

At Toby's house, everyone gathered indoors and it wasn't long before laughter and singing could be heard at the other end of the street.

* * *

Heady with success, Clarice had been plotting her next attack on the casinos of Birmingham. She could think of no other way to do it other than what she'd done at Monty's. That endeavour had proved successful so, rolling up a newspaper, she had waited for darkness to descend. Setting out, she purchased half a bottle of brandy and a box of matches from a liquor shop on her way. It would be useful as an accelerant, and if it wasn't needed, she could always drink it.

Again, with furtive glances around her, she shot into the shadows behind the building. Lights blazed in what she assumed to be the kitchen. Damn and blast! Clearly it was still in use, which meant she would have to wait in the cold until the lights went out.

These places were open twenty-four hours a day and provided food and hot drinks to those who wanted to continue playing rather than break off in search of a meal.

The cold nipped her toes despite the woollen socks she wore but she dared not stamp her feet for fear of being seen or heard. She wriggled her toes inside her boots until she felt them warm up a little. Her gloved hands were pushed deep into her pockets, her drawstring bag hanging heavily over her arm.

'Come on, you buggers!' she whispered. 'Hurry the hell up!'

For over an hour, she waited, and just when she was about to give up and go home, the lights went out. Eager to be about her business then be gone, Clarice held on to her patience and waited five more minutes in case anyone returned to the room.

Creeping to the door, she tried the handle. Cursing inwardly at finding it locked, she moved back to the shadows. Now what?

Taking out the brandy, she pulled the cork. What the hell, she took a swig and had to stifle the cough that rose to her throat. Feeling the burn as the alcohol went down, she smiled. *Good choice, Clarice!*

Sidling up to the door once more, she unrolled the newspaper and sprinkled some brandy onto it. Then she pushed it under the door. Throwing more brandy at the door, she struck a match, and cupping her hands around the tiny flame, she touched it to the edges of the paper. With a sudden whoosh, the alcohol on the door caught alight. Clarice jumped back out of its reach and watched a moment as the door soon began to glow. It was beginning to burn – time to go. She shoved the cork back in the bottle, then pushed it into her bag as she strode away into a fairly quiet street.

Nobody took any notice of the woman hurrying along in a bid to be out of the cold.

Ten minutes later, a woman screamed, 'Fire!' and people fought to get out of the premises which were now firmly ablaze.

Clarice packed her belongings as soon as she got back to the hotel. Taking her key to the reception, she paid her bill and left. Now she had to find lodgings for a couple of nights because she had decided there was one more casino to dispense with. Three would have to be enough because the more she pushed her luck, the likelihood of getting caught rose. After that, she would board a train headed for London. The bright casino lights of the capital were calling to her and she could resist no longer.

41

Jared and Rose took a cab home. It was late when they left Ivy Lane and it was freezing. Once indoors, Jared got the range going and sat Rose in front of its open doors.

Rose watched him bustle about making tea. *He's nervous*, she thought, *but so am I.*

'Jared, maybe we should just go up,' she said.

'Yes, of course, if you want. You go on and I'll be along when I've made the house safe. It's the room on the left.'

Rose lit the oil lamp and made her way to the bedroom.

Jared paced the kitchen. 'Oh, God!' he whispered. 'This is it. I have to... perform!' He dragged a hand through his hair then straightened his shoulders. 'Stop piddling about and get on with it!'

Closing the range and locking the doors, Jared climbed the stairs in the dark. The door was ajar and the lamplight spilled out onto the tiny landing.

Clearing his throat to let Rose know he was on his way, Jared stepped into the room. He saw her wedding dress hanging on the wardrobe door and he looked at her in his bed. She had the bedclothes pulled up to her chin and she was shivering.

'Hurry up, I'm perished!' she called out.

With no more ado, Jared stripped off his clothes and climbed in beside her. Both naked beneath the covers, they clung to each other for warmth. *Nothing will happen here tonight if I don't get bloody warm!*

Jared kissed his young bride and she returned it with fervour. Slowly, gently they explored each other's bodies, the heat building between them. Jared cupped her breast and heard her tiny gasp. He traced his fingers over to the other one and again Rose's breath sounded close to his ear. Down her body his hand went and as he touched her most intimate place, Rose whispered, 'Now, Jared.'

Rolling onto her, he entered her as gently as he could, aware of her hands on his back. He began to build up a steady rhythm until cries from them both shattered the silence. Sweat covered their bodies and as he moved to her side, he panted, 'Did I hurt you? I'm sorry if I did.'

'Only for a moment but then it was... bliss.'

Jared smiled at her and she giggled. 'This feels so naughty!'

'I know, but it's allowed now we're married,' Jared said, feeling rather proud of himself.

They laughed together before another kiss began to rekindle their passion once more.

* * *

Clarice entered a shabby boarding house and paid for one night's stay. She was shown to a room which was a far cry from the Midland Hotel. There was no fire in the hearth and nothing with which to build one. She was given the key and left to her own devices.

Setting her bag on the bed, she sat down beside it. The bedstead creaked and Clarice sighed. *One more day and I'll be gone from this city*, she thought, which cheered her a little.

She lay down on the lumpy mattress; she didn't bother to undress. Not sure how clean the sheets were, she decided to sleep on top of the bed. She wondered how much of the casino had actually burned as she lay there, her eyes on the cracked ceiling. It didn't really matter because she'd done what she set out to do. If the last one went as well she'd be more than happy, and she'd be long gone before the police could find out who was setting the fires.

Remembering there was a little brandy left in the bottle, she got up and fished it out of her bag. Pulling out the cork, she drank the remainder. The empty bottle she stood on the dressing table then lay back on the bed again. With a huge satisfied sigh, Clarice drifted off to sleep, safe in the knowledge she would soon be playing her beloved cards once more.

* * *

Jared and Rose slept in the following morning. Jared was about to climb out of bed when Rose pulled him back. With a grin, he acquiesced to her wishes and it was an hour later that he finally rose.

By the time Rose came downstairs, the range was glowing, filling the kitchen with a cosy warmth. Rose busied herself getting to know her way around and cooking breakfast.

Jared watched her slim form and his heart swelled with love and pride. He still couldn't believe he was a married man.

'If there's anything you wish to change in the house, it's all right with me,' he said.

'No, I'm more than happy with what we have,' Rose answered as she presented him with his morning meal. 'I'll make the bed once we've eaten.'

'I'll help,' Jared said with a twinkle in his eye.

Rose's laughter filled the room. 'We'll not get much done at this rate.'

'Who cares?' Jared said before he tucked into his bacon and eggs.

* * *

Clarice was up early, she needed to buy another newspaper and more brandy. The paper would give her the details about how well her arson attack had gone before it would be used in the next. What she didn't know was whether the police could already be on to her. After the fire which burned Monty's to the ground, the police had questioned as many people as could be found who had attended the place.

It was one man, however, who gave them a good lead which they felt needed following up on. Anthony Purcell had visited his friend, Inspector Nicholas Cameron, and told him the tale of Clarice Connaught aka Clara Christian. The inspector had agreed that being banned from the casino could well have sparked Clarice's anger, but he questioned whether it would result in such a diabolical act. He promised to have the lady brought in for interview. Before that could happen, however, there had been another fire and his men were busy searching for witnesses yet again.

Information came in dribs and drabs; people had seen a

woman walking away from the area at the time but they were unable to identify her. It was dark and they didn't take that much notice, thinking the woman was just another pedestrian eager to be home out of the freezing temperature.

Purcell had said that Clarice had been staying at the Midland Hotel but when a bobby had been sent there, the woman had gone. That was where the lead went cold.

Inspector Cameron was not a man to give up and he called a meeting of his officers. A large map of Birmingham was pinned to the wall in his office at the station and red circles adorned it.

'These are the casinos that we are aware of and each one could be the location of the next arson attack.'

'Are we sure there will be one, sir?' a voice sounded from the back of the room.

'Not sure, no, but it's a fairly safe bet. I'm given to understand it could be a woman we're after; one who has been banned from these places on suspicion of cheating.'

A buzz went round the room as the constables murmured to each other.

'All right, settle down. Now, I think she'll try again, although which of these she'll choose...' the inspector slapped the map with a wooden pointing stick, 'is anyone's guess. So, for the next few nights, I want pairs stationed at each of these venues.'

A groan went up at the thought of having to stand in the cold all night, at least walking the beat helped to keep them warm.

'I know, lads, but maybe this will make it worthwhile. At Monty's, everyone managed to get out before the fire really took hold. However, at the fire last evening, a woman, a waitress, was trapped inside and burned to death.' The inspector watched as shivers rippled around the room. 'Not a nice way to go, eh?' After seeing their heads shake, he went on. 'Therefore we are hunting not only an arsonist but also a murderer.' He paused again to allow his words to sink in. 'The sergeant will assign you your duties. Be vigilant, lads; let's catch this bugger before she strikes again! Dismissed.'

42

Clarice read the few words she could make out in the article on
the front page of the newspaper and gasped. She had thought
there was more than enough time for everyone to get out before
the building was razed to the ground. Evidently some stupid
woman had managed to get herself trapped and in doing so had
lost her life.

'It's your own fault,' Clarice whispered into the quiet of her
dingy room, 'you should have legged it quicker. It's not my fault
you were too slow.' Refusing to accept the blame, Clarice nevertheless shivered as she tried to read the piece again. In pure frustration, she threw the paper down.

She did wonder, but only for a moment, whether she should
cut her losses and flee now. Then she thought how humiliated
she had felt at being refused entry at the casinos and her blood
boiled. 'One more then I'm gone.'

Her clothes were still in the Gladstone bag and she considered taking it with her but realised it would be cumbersome. If
she paid for one more night at the boarding house, she could

leave it here. She didn't have to stay the whole night, she could retrieve her bag after the deed was done and then disappear.

Going to the reception, she paid for another night's stay then returned to her room to wait until dark. Rolling up her money, she hid it in her chemise. That way, if something should go wrong, she would have the means to flee immediately. Her bag she could afford to lose and her clothes could be replaced.

Ennui set in and Clarice paced the room. She had looked over the newspaper from cover to cover, trying to make out more of the words, but to no avail. With nothing more to do, she decided to go out for something to eat.

Finding a café not too far away, she ordered cottage pie and vegetables and a pot of tea. Sitting by the window, she watched the people passing by. She caught sight of a couple of constables strolling along chatting. *Odd, they usually patrol alone*, she thought. However, it was dismissed from her mind the moment her food arrived. By the time she had finished eating, darkness had already begun to fall. Paying her bill, she left the café. Stopping only to purchase another half bottle of brandy, Clarice returned to her room to retrieve the items she needed, then she set out once more on the path of destruction.

Reaching her destination, Clarice stood across the road, looking at the building she was planning to burn down. A strange feeling crept over her, as though she was being watched, but she couldn't see anyone staring as she glanced around her. The street was deserted which felt surreal in such a busy city. Then she remembered she was out earlier this evening; folk would be home having their dinner.

Clarice waited and looked around, she couldn't shake off the feeling of having eyes on her. She debated whether to leave it and go, but the memories of being banned rose in her again, fuelling her anger.

Stepping across the road, Clarice moved quickly into the shadows. Pulling out the brandy, she sloshed it up the door before re-corking the bottle and dropping it into her bag.

The two policemen standing silently further back, hiding behind a bush, glanced at each other by the light of the moon. They watched as Clarice slid sheets of newspaper into the gap beneath the door. Then, as she struck a match, they pounced. The match fell to the floor and was immediately extinguished by the cobbles still wet from a rain shower.

'Get off me!' Clarice yelled as she struggled to release herself from the two men holding her arms.

'Madam, you are under arrest for attempted arson,' one constable said as they marched her away to the front of the building. Handcuffs had been attached to her wrists and Clarice knew the game was up. The other constable knocked on the door and informed the doorman about what they had seen. 'Please leave everything as it is until the inspector has been to have a look. Also ensure everyone stays indoors as the inspector may want to speak with them.'

The shocked doorman nodded before closing the door again.

Clarice was marched to the police station. The red brick building had railings covering the ground-floor windows and a blue glass lamp hung over the doorway.

She was taken inside and was booked in at the front desk by the sergeant before being ushered through a door and down some stairs. Here she was placed in a cell with concrete walls measuring around eight feet by five feet. A small window with bars was set high up in one wall. A straw pallet sat on a concrete shelf for a bed and a bucket in the corner served as a toilet facility. Her handcuffs were removed and the sturdy iron-grilled door was slammed shut behind her and locked securely. The policemen walked away and Clarice heard their footsteps receding as they ascended the stairs and closed the door at the top. Clarice sat on the bed wearily. She was alone but not afraid. She had committed the crime and now she would have to do the time. She was resigned to the fact that she would spend time in jail, after which she would be released and allowed to go her own way once more.

The two policemen in the room above the cells gave an account of the events to Inspector Cameron.

'Well done, lads! Caught her red-handed.'

'We told 'em as to leave the scene untouched until you'd seen it for yerself, guv,' one said.

'Good, I'll do that now before I interview little Miss Firestarter. You two come with me.' The inspector and the two bobbies went off to inspect the scene of the crime then returned to the station.

Clarice was brought from her cell to a room to answer some questions.

'Now then, what's your name?'

'Clarice Connaught.'

'Do you also go by the name of Clara Christian?'

'I have at times.'

'Can you tell me what you were doing tonight at the back of that casino?'

'I was trying to get inside.'

'Why go round the back? Why didn't you go in the front entrance?'

'Because I was banned!' Clarice snapped.

'I see. Then can you please explain why my constables saw you pour alcohol on the door then strike a match close to it?'

Clarice realised she had been caught red-handed and had no other choice but to own up.

'I was about to burn it down,' she said quietly.

The admission took Cameron and the constables by surprise. They had thought she would continue to deny her actions, ranting and raving but no, here she was confessing to all.

'Can you write a statement for us?'

'No, I can't read or write very well.'

'Then I shall have someone write down your words as you tell it.' Cameron sent for another constable who bustled in with notepad and pen. He listened in silence as Clarice related her tale. At the end, he asked, 'Do you have any kin?'

'My father, John Connaught. He lives in Erskine Street.'

The Inspector turned to one of the bobbies and said, 'Fetch him.' Returning his attention to Clarice, he said, 'A woman died in one of the fires you set.'

'I know,' Clarice answered calmly.

'So you will be charged with murder as well as arson.' Clarice shrugged and said nothing. Inspector Cameron sighed loudly. 'Do you feel no remorse for what you've done?'

'No. Why should I?' Now Clarice's temper was beginning to rise.

'You killed a woman!' Cameron boomed.

'No, I didn't, the fire killed that woman. Besides, she should have got out earlier,' Clarice countered.

'The law states—'

'I don't give a bugger what the law says, I'm telling you to let me out of this place *now!*'

The inspector leaned back in his chair at her outburst. She had been compliant when they brought her in, then in an instant she had changed into a very angry young woman.

'Fetch some tea, maybe that will calm her down,' he instructed the secretarial constable as he took the notebook and placed it on the table before him.

'I don't want tea! I want out of here!' Clarice yelled into his face as she got to her feet.

'Well, that's not going to happen, so sit your arse down.' The inspector kept his voice low and even.

Clarice dropped back onto the chair with a growl.

'Now then, it says here you set the door on fire using brandy as an accelerant.' Cameron looked at her for confirmation.

'I have no idea what you're talking about.'

Another sigh escaped the inspector's lips. So this was how she wanted to play it. Confess and retract, a good old coppers' and felons' game; one Inspector Cameron was good at and he had never lost yet.

'All right, let's start again.'

43

Whilst Clarice's father was being brought to the station, Alice McGuire asked her husband, 'Are you all right, sweetheart?' as he climbed out of bed.

'To be sure, *mavourneen*, I'm thirsty so I'll go and make a cuppa. You stay there and I'll bring one up to you.'

It was in the early hours of the morning and chilly, so Alice snuggled down beneath the blankets once more. She smiled to herself, thinking how lucky she was to have been able to marry Toby McGuire after all the years of waiting to do just that. Slowly her eyelids drooped as sleep tried to claim her again.

Suddenly her eyes snapped open as she realised Toby had not returned to bed. Whatever was he doing down in the cold kitchen? Slipping from the warmth of the blankets, Alice threw on her dressing-gown, a present from Toby for her birthday, and made her way downstairs.

'Toby?' she called out. She saw the gas lamps lit and headed straight for the kitchen. What she found took her breath away.

Toby was lying on the floor clutching his chest. Alice rushed to him. 'Toby! Oh, my God!'

She could see that his face was drained of colour and he was sweating. Alice tried to help him up but he seemed like a dead weight. He was panting and his face was screwed up in pain.

'Jesus Christ! Oh, Toby, I need to get help!'

'No,' Toby gasped. 'Too late.'

'Bugger that, I'm fetching the doctor!' Alice turned to leave the house but Toby's groan of pain had her turn back to him.

'Alice...' he said in barely more than a whisper. '*Mavourneen...*'

'I'm here, we have to get you up, Toby, then I can go for the doctor!' Alice was beside herself with worry.

'Alice...'

Sitting on the floor, she cradled Toby's head in her lap as tears rolled down her face.

'I've... always... loved you... Alice,' Toby managed.

'I've always loved you an' all, Toby, but please... I must fetch the doctor!'

'Kiss me, Alice... one last time.' Toby's eyes looked longingly into hers.

'Don't you dare say that!' Alice shifted his head from her lap and lay down beside him. 'You ain't going nowhere, you bugger! One kiss then it's up on your feet, do you hear me?'

Toby managed a small nod of the head. 'I love you, Alice McGuire.'

Alice perched herself on one elbow and leaned over to kiss her beloved husband. The kiss lingered and as she pulled back, she realised he had passed from this world. With a deep breath, Alice lay down again, her head on his shoulder, her arm wrapped over his body as if trying to keep him safe. There she stayed, crying her heart out until the cold grey light of the morning began to creep in through the window.

Eventually Alice was able to pull herself together enough to get dressed. She donned her coat and boots and set out for the undertakers. Grateful that the funeral parlour was manned night and day, she hurried inside.

'I need you to come, my husband...'

'Steady, missus,' the man said as he helped her to a chair. 'Where do you live?'

'Ivy Lane, it's Toby McGuire.'

'Oh, wench, I'm sorry to hear it. Has the doctor been?'

Alice shook her head. 'I never thought...'

'No matter.' The man picked up the telephone so recently installed and was connected to the doctor's house.

'Thank you, we'll meet you there. The doctor is coming, so let's get you home.' Ringing a little bell on the desk, he waited whilst two other men appeared. 'Mr McGuire, Ivy Lane,' he said. Then to Alice, 'Come, Mrs McGuire, you can ride with me.'

Helped aboard the cart, Alice rode home in silence apart from the occasional sob. They arrived at the same time as the doctor who Alice showed into the kitchen.

'He was gasping and holding his chest,' Alice cried.

'Heart attack would be my guess, I'm so sorry, Mrs McGuire.' Writing out a certificate and handing it to her, the doctor left.

Alice watched as her husband was lifted into a transportation coffin. 'He's all paid up,' she whispered.

'Very good. When you're able, come and see us to make the arrangements.'

Alice nodded. It was only after they had taken her Toby away that Alice was undone. She howled her despair into the empty kitchen, sounding for all the world like a wounded animal. She cried until she had no more tears then she sat staring at the floor for the remainder of the pre-dawn hours.

* * *

Over at the police station, Clarice Connaught was also howling, but in anger. 'Why have you brought him here?' she yelled, pointing to her father.

'Clarice, girl, what's happened to you? What have you come to that you should do such terrible things?'

'Bugger off! I ain't talking to you!'

'Now then, miss, let's not get all riled up again,' Inspector Cameron said.

'You can bugger off an' all!' Clarice snapped.

A young constable brought in a cup of tea and placed it in front of Clarice. Like a shot, she was out of her chair and leapt onto the policeman. Before he could react, she took his earlobe in her teeth and pulled. Blood spurted and the constable screamed in pain. Clarice spat out the earlobe and began to laugh maniacally.

'Oh, Christ! Get him up to the hospital sharpish,' Cameron said as he leapt to his feet, 'and send me two more officers – hurry up!'

John Connaught stared in horror at his daughter, at the blood dripping down her chin as she laughed. *Dear God, whatever has gone wrong with you, Clarice?*

'Stay away or you'll be next!' Clarice shouted as two more constables came into the room. Despite her handcuffs, Clarice was a force to be reckoned with, seething with anger and indignation.

'Right, you two, get her back into the cells, she'll be up before the magistrate in the morning, and watch yourselves 'cos she's already injured Constable Bluck.'

The two young officers exchanged a glance then stepped towards Clarice.

'Argh!' she bellowed as she launched herself, but the policemen were ready for it and had her by the arms before she could do any more damage. They dragged her away kicking and screaming that she would get even with the casinos as soon as she was released. 'They won't get away with it, you'll see! I'll 'ave 'em begging me to go back! Let me go, you swine!'

'I'm sorry, Mr Connaught, I thought seeing you might calm her down. Evidently I was wrong,' Cameron said.

'Why is she here?' John asked, still in shock at what he'd witnessed.

'I'm sorry to have to inform you that we believe she is the arsonist, Mr Connaught. We caught her in the process of lighting another fire at a casino.'

'Why?'

'Apparently it's because they banned her for cheating at cards.'

'Inspector, Clarice has never cheated at cards in her life, she's inordinately good. So good she doesn't have to cheat,' John said in disbelief.

'Well, I'm afraid they thought otherwise and here we are. I suggest you go home and try to get some rest. Thank you for coming in.'

'What will happen to her now?' John asked.

'She'll be up before the magistrate in the morning then he'll decide what's to be done with her.'

'Will she go to jail, Inspector?'

'My guess would be yes. Arson is a serious crime, Mr Connaught, and now she has attacked and mutilated a police officer on duty.' The inspector gave a small sympathetic shrug.

'Thank you.' John nodded and left, walking as if in a stupor.

Cameron yelled, 'Can someone bring a mop and bucket and clean this bloody mess up, please?'

Clarice bawled and banged around in the cell all night and

by morning, Inspector Cameron had a headache that threatened to split his head in two.

* * *

As the morning light filtered through the window, Alice McGuire got to her feet mechanically. She trudged over to the yard and was greeted by the Cavenors.

'Alice?' Bobby asked, surprised to see her, for Alice never came to their place of work.

'Bobby, Toby's gone.'

'Gone where, love?'

'Gone to the Lord,' she replied wearily.

'Oh, dear God, no! Alice, I'm so sorry.' Bobby wrapped an arm around Alice as she swayed on her feet.

'What you sorry for? Oh, hello, Alice,' Dicky said.

'Toby's passed on,' Bobby said.

'Bugger me, I thought he'd live forever!' Dicky said.

Suddenly Alice began to laugh, which quickly turned to heart-wrenching sobs.

Bobby called Tim over. 'Fetch Jared, Toby's died.'

With a curt nod and a glum expression, Tim raced off.

The brothers took Alice to sit by the fire in the office and made her some tea. 'Jared won't be long,' Bobby reassured her.

Alice stared at the cup in her hand and Bobby and Dicky shared a worried look. They had no idea what to say, so they kept quiet. Grief was slowly creeping up on them as the shock began to wear off and neither wanted to break down in front of Alice.

Tim banged on Jared's back door, yelling his son's name.

'Hey up, Dad, what's going on?' Jared asked as he opened the door.

'You have... to come... Toby's passed,' Tim panted.

'Oh, God!' Jared crumpled and Tim caught him and took him to a chair.

'Tim?' Rose said, coming into the kitchen and seeing Jared bawling his eyes out.

Tim explained quickly and Rose knelt before her husband. 'Jared, my love, you have to go because Alice will be depending on you now.'

Wiping away his tears, Jared kissed her and grabbed his coat. He and his father hurried back to the yard. As he entered the office, Alice stood and put the cup on the desk.

Jared went to her and wrapped his arms around her. The two wept for the big Irishman whom they had both loved dearly.

The Cavenor brothers held onto each other as their tears finally fell. The man who had been their boss for many years and treated them like gents had gone.

Work in the yard had stopped, the sorters' bewildered looks passing from one to another. It was Tim who explained what all the commotion was about and they all removed their caps in respect.

'Mr Bobby, summon a cab, please,' Jared managed at last. 'I'm taking Alice home.'

'Yes, Boss,' came the strangled reply. The two big brothers were struggling as they tried to keep their emotions in check.

'Seth needs to know,' Alice said as Jared led her towards the cab. 'He loved my Toby for rescuing him from his cruel father.'

'I know and I'll see to it. First, let's get you home.'

'He loved you like a son, Jared, did my Toby.'

Jared's tears sprang forth at the words. 'I loved him too, Alice,' he said amid his sobs.

44

Across town, Clarice had been transported to the Victoria Law Court in Birmingham and was being dragged before the magistrate. The impressive red brick building had two tall towers either side of an arched entrance and looked more like a castle than a courthouse.

The magistrate sat behind a huge desk dressed in a dark suit covered by a black flowing gown with a wing collar. On his head sat a short curly wig.

Up in the gallery, the seats were full of people gawking at the woman now stood in the dock, a policeman standing either side of her. Many people enjoyed the spectacle of the court process and were allowed into the gallery to hear the cases. Unemployed men in jackets and flat caps and women in their best hats sat eagerly waiting to discover what this young woman was accused of. Some had brought picnics to see them through the morning.

The clerk read out the charges. 'Miss Clarice Connaught, caught by two policemen setting fire to the casino in Lawrence Street. Miss Connaught admitted arson at two other casinos resulting in the death of one Gladys Rowbottom, a waitress.'

Cries of *murderer!* rang out across the court room and bits of food were thrown at Clarice. She glared at the people screaming at her from their vantage point high up on the walls of the court room.

Banging his gavel for quiet, the magistrate looked around the room as he waited patiently for the noise to die down.

Then he nodded. 'Sounds cut and dried to me. Miss Connaught, you will be incarcerated at Stafford Gaol until such time as your trial takes place and henceforth sentenced by a High Court judge. Next!' Down came the gavel again with a sharp bang.

Clarice snarled as she was hauled away to be transported to prison.

John Connaught sat in the court room and sobbed his sorrow into a handkerchief. His daughter would be jailed for the rest of her life for what she had done. As he left the building, he wondered if the fault lay with him for teaching her how to play cards in the first place. No, he resigned himself to the fact that Clarice had a black heart and that no matter how hard he'd tried with her, she would have ended up exactly where she was now.

She had shown no remorse for taking that poor girl's life, and John had to agree that the longer she was locked away, the safer people would be. Despite all that had happened, there was a part of him that still loved his daughter and always would.

* * *

Alice had thought she was all cried out but as she explained everything to Jared when they sat in the kitchen at Ivy Lane, her tears fell again.

'Alice, this has come as a shock to us all,' Jared said quietly.

'Ar, I know, lad, to me especially. Toby was in good health or so I thought,' she answered, drying her eyes on her handkerchief.

Going to the bureau, she had pulled out both of their funeral plans.

'Toby paid them up in full so we wouldn't have to worry,' she said, passing them to Jared.

'I'll see to it for you,' he said.

'Will you see to mine an' all when the time comes?'

'I will.'

'I trust you more than my sons, they're just after the money they think might come their way.'

'You mustn't fret, I'll deal with everything.'

'The solicitor has his will, I have to go...'

'I'll come with you. Do you want to go now? We might have to make an appointment, though.'

Nodding, Alice got to her feet. 'I need to know if I have to leave this place.'

'You won't, not if I know that husband of yours.'

Hailing a cab, he and Alice were taken to the solicitor's office where Jared explained why they were there. The man gave his condolences, saying he could see them right then and there, before diving into a large cupboard set into the wall.

Opening the document, he said, 'Yes, here we are. Toby McGuire.' Going to the door, he called in his secretary and his partner in the business. 'Mrs McGuire, meet Miss Stewart and Mr Clancy, they witnessed your husband's will at the time of making it.'

Alice nodded as they too gave their condolences at her sad loss.

'I will read this out in the presence of the two witnesses. I, Toby McGuire, being of sound mind, erm... Yes, here it says, to my wife, Alice, I leave the house in Ivy Lane and the sum of two and a half thousand pounds.'

Alice gasped. 'Two and a half thou… I didn't know he had so much money!'

The solicitor went on. 'To my manager, Jared Johnson, I leave the business and the sum of one thousand pounds.'

Now it was Jared's turn to gasp.

'To Seth Watkins, Bobby Cavenor and Dicky Cavenor, five hundred pounds each.'

'I'm glad he remembered Seth,' Alice said quietly.

'That just about covers it,' the solicitor said.

'He left nothing to my boys?' Alice asked.

'It would appear not,' the solicitor said as he scanned the document again.

'I'm glad. They don't deserve a penny.'

The solicitor looked from Alice to Jared, questions showing on his face.

'They treated me badly, so Toby did the right thing to my mind.'

'Once we hear back from the probate office, you will be able to access the monies from the estate.'

'Does that mean that Mrs McGuire can stay in the house in the meantime?' Jared asked.

'Yes indeed, I'm sorry, I should have made that clear,' the solicitor said.

Giving their thanks, Jared took Alice home in the waiting cab.

'You'll need to change the name of the business now, lad,' Alice said as they entered the house.

'No, I'm going to leave it as it is out of respect and love for the big man.'

'He'd be proud, so he would,' Alice said, then added, 'Hark at me talking like him. They say live with them and you get like them.'

Jared chuckled and before long both were laughing loudly. Despite the sadness of the occasion, it was just what they both needed.

Before he left her to go to the yard, Jared asked, 'Will you be all right, Alice?'

'Ar, lad, you get off, I'll be fine.' The lie almost choked her because Alice knew she would never be the same again. She had waited a lifetime for Toby McGuire and after five short years had lost him again – this time for good.

Jared left Ivy Lane and hurried over to the yard.

'How's Alice doing, Boss?' Bobby asked.

'As you would expect, Mr Bobby. Could you both spare me a minute in the office please?'

The brothers followed Jared and it was then that he asked them to take a seat.

'I've just returned from the solicitor's office with Alice. It seems that Mr McGuire has remembered everyone in his will. He has left you each five hundred pounds which you will receive once probate has gone through.'

'Well, bugger me!' Dicky exclaimed.

'I was thinking the same thing, bro,' Bobby said.

'The yard has come to me and Alice gets the house plus money to see her right.' It was not his place to divulge the amount but they needed to know that Alice would be safe in her house, as well as what was happening with the business.

The brothers nodded, seemingly nonplussed by their good fortune. Both would, as would Jared and Alice, have given it all up to have Toby back amongst the living.

'The yard will close on the day of the funeral; I'll let everyone know when that is.' Jared was keeping his grief at bay by trying to stay busy. 'I'm going over to the bank to inform the manager and sort out anything that needs doing there. Then I'll come back ready for when the lads get back.'

Once he had gone, Bobby and Dicky stood around the brazier, still hardly able to believe Toby had gone.

'It was bloody nice of him to remember us in his will,' Dicky said quietly so only his brother could hear.

'Yeah,' was all that Bobby could manage for fear of his emotions overwhelming him.

An hour later and Jared was back.

'How did you get on, Boss?' Bobby asked.

'The manager is aware and will sort everything out after probate comes through. I've arranged for a telephone to be installed both here and at Ivy Lane, that way if Alice needs us she can just call.'

'Good idea,' Dicky said.

'I'll just run across home and let Rose know what's going on. I'll see you in a bit.' Jared left the brothers and legged it across the heath. He arrived to find Rose donning her outdoor clothes.

'I'm going to be with Alice for a while,' she said.

'Thanks, sweetheart, I hated having to leave her but I had important arrangements to see to.'

'I know. I'll stay with her for the rest of today and come back home this evening.'

'Can you tell her a telephone is being installed at her house and also in the yard in case she needs us? Take a cab there and back 'cos I don't want you on the heath in the dark.'

Rose kissed her new husband and left the house.

Jared dropped onto a kitchen chair and allowed his feelings to finally be released. His body shook as he sobbed his woes into the silence of the room. Anger at having yet another loved one taken before their time raged through him. The sadness of not being able to talk and laugh with Toby any more tore at his heart. His wail of despair echoed through the house and out across the scrubland. Jared Johnson was in tremendous pain and anyone within hearing distance would know it. Jared cried until his chest ached and his tears dried up and only then did he feel able to carry on.

45

Clarice screamed with rage all the way to Stafford Gaol in the prison carriage. On arrival, she was booked in by a hard-faced woman then taken to a cell she would be sharing with another inmate. There she was searched for any weapons she might be concealing and her shackles were removed, then the door banged shut, the key rasping in the lock.

Eyeing the other woman lying on her bed, Clarice moved to sit on her own.

'Welcome to paradise. My name is Sadie Entwhistle. What you in for?'

Clarice introduced herself and explained a little of her story.

A moment later, the key rattled in the lock and a warder, who Clarice would have sworn was a man in a dress, called out, 'Connaught! With me!'

Clarice rose to her feet and followed the warder and saw she was being led to the shower room. 'Get your clothes off, get washed then put these on.'

Clarice was handed a rough grey woollen dress, a pair of woollen stockings and cotton drawers and chemise. The warder picked up Clarice's clothes and retrieved the roll of money which had tumbled out of her chemise.

'Hey, that belongs to me!'

'Not any more it doesn't,' the warder said as she pocketed the notes. 'Remember, Connaught, you lost all your rights when you came in here. Now get a move on!'

Clarice was livid that this woman had stolen her money and would probably not be reprimanded for it. She growled with disgust as she stepped beneath the shower. The water was freezing cold and Clarice's breath caught in her throat, her temper rose again as she heard the warder laugh nastily at her shivering under the spray which made her teeth chatter.

When she was washed and dressed, her own clothes were thrown into a massive basket before she was pushed forward into another room. Here her hair was shorn, leaving her with a bristly scalp. Clarice forced herself not to cry at the loss of her beautiful dark locks. Now she resembled every other inmate. She was returned to her cell, feeling absolutely wretched.

'You'll work tomorrow when the guv'nor finds summat for you to do,' the warder said before locking her in once more.

Inwardly Clarice cursed her father for ever teaching her how to play cards, Clifford for introducing her into the casino fraternity and herself for not leaving Birmingham when she had the chance.

Sadie told Clarice that she had been apprehended for killing her bully of a husband. 'He struck me once too often and I snapped. I flew at him with the carving knife and stabbed him in the heart. I watched the bastard die right in front of me. The coppers arrived 'cos my bloody nosy neighbour dobbed me in when she heard all the noise. It ruined me knife to boot! So, here I am – for the rest of me life.' She sighed loudly and stretched out her legs.

Clarice shuddered as realisation settled upon her. She too would spend her remaining days in this hell-hole. Finally the emotions got the better of her as tears rolled down her face and she sobbed.

'It ain't no use crying now, wench. You did the crime, now you have to do the time. Besides, you don't want to appear weak in here 'cos they'll eat you for breakfast.'

Clarice dried her eyes on her sleeve. Sadie was right, she had to be strong otherwise she would wither and die like a flower in winter.

'I'll show you the ropes and tell you who to watch out for. There's folks comin' and goin' all the time here so we don't get much rest. They work you bloody hard an' all and – the food is shit!' Clarice felt her resolve begin to crumble again as Sadie prattled on. 'You need to work in the kitchen if you can 'cos the laundry is a nightmare. I've seen hands cracked and bleeding from working in there and the warders don't give a damn.'

The more Sadie talked, the more fearful Clarice became. 'I have to get out of here!' Clarice said desperately.

Sadie laughed. 'Oh, girl, there ain't no getting out of this place once you're sentenced, unless it's in a box!'

Clarice's mind began to whirl. *I have to be taken to court for trial. That would be my chance to attempt an escape. I don't know how but I have to try.*

After the worst days of her life, Clarice was shackled, wrists and ankles. She was then transported to the Victorian Law Court in Birmingham once more by two burly female warders. There was no chance of escape and Clarice knew it. She shuffled into the court room and was pushed into the dock.

The judge in his black robes and curly wig entered and, sitting behind his huge desk, he peered down at her. The case was being put before the judge by a lawyer Clarice had never met. He was arguing that she was not of sound mind at the time of the crime because of being banned unjustly from the casinos. Another lawyer argued back, saying Clarice knew exactly what she was doing and had started the fires deliberately in retribution.

Clarice was terrified of the shouting and disagreements by the men dressed in black with their curly wigs so she slipped into a world of her own where she felt she was safe.

'Clarice Connaught, do you have anything to say before I pass sentence?' the judge asked.

Clarice jumped at the sound of her name. 'I... I wasn't cheating at cards, if only they'd have let me explain...'

'You are not here because of cheating at cards, you are here because of your arson attacks, one of which took the life of a young woman!'

Clarice lowered her eyes and nodded. He was right, of course. She was sorry the woman had died but as for the fires... she felt no remorse in starting them.

'So be it. Clarice Connaught, you are sentenced to life imprisonment for murder and arson. You will be taken from here to a place of incarceration to live out the remainder of your days.' The judge stood and, in a flurry of black robes looking like fluttering crows' wings, he left the courtroom.

Up in the gallery, John Connaught was breaking his heart. He had been shocked when he saw his daughter brought into court. She was pale with dark circles beneath her eyes, and her hair! They had cut it so short he could see her scalp. He barely recognised her in the prison clothes and he could not prevent his hand from covering his mouth to silence the sob caught in his throat.

Clarice was pushed out of the room and locked inside the

transport carriage once more. She felt like she was in a trance and couldn't quite understand what was happening to her.

John left the court, knowing he would never see his girl again. He would not visit her in prison because he knew she would not want to see him, and it would hurt him so much knowing she was never to be released he might never get over it. He went home a broken man.

At the prison, Clarice was unshackled and led onto her landing. Shoved into her cell, now empty as Sadie was working, Clarice winced when the warder grabbed her breast and squeezed. 'You're all mine now and for as long as I want you!'

The warder laughed loudly before slamming the door and locking it soundly.

Clarice shivered. She knew exactly what the warder had meant and her stomach roiled at the thought. As she sat on her bed and her tears fell again, she thought, *You touch me again and I'll kill you!*

That night, Clarice covered her ears to the sound of wailing echoing through the otherwise quiet prison. Hundreds of women were housed here and most were of the same opinion – they were innocent.

Clarice heard the key turn in the lock and she opened her eyes to see a dark shadow approach her bed.

'I told you, you're mine now,' the warder said in a harsh whisper, before laying her lips on Clarice's.

Clarice leapt from her bed, shoving the woman away from her. 'You stay away from me, you filthy beast!'

'Or what?' the warder sneered.

'Or I'll scream my head off!'

'It won't do you no good, 'cos I'm in charge of this landing, see!' The warder stepped forward to grab Clarice, intending to throw her onto the bed once more.

Clarice, however, had other ideas and grabbing the night-soil bucket she swung it at the warder's head. Urine sprayed everywhere but Clarice didn't care. The warder went down and Clarice jumped on top of her, banging the bucket repeatedly against the other woman's head. The warder tried to struggle and scream but her senses had left her and her efforts were in vain.

A red mist had enveloped Clarice and she didn't give up until the warder stopped moving. By the light of the moon, Clarice saw what she had done. The warder's face was smashed to a bloody pulp and her chest no longer rose and fell. Clarice had committed murder for the second time.

As Clarice dropped to sit on her bed, she saw Sadie watching her. The bedclothes were pulled up to her chin and only her eyes were visible in the silvery moonlight.

When Sadie asked, 'What are we going to piss in now?' Clarice's laughter resounded out along the landing, the broken bucket still in her hand.

46

The commotion in the cell had roused the other prisoners who set to howling again and banging until the gas lamps lit up the area.

Two warders found Clarice clutching the bucket, covered in blood and laughing like a lunatic. Their colleague was lying dead on the floor at her feet.

'Bloody hell!' one gasped.

'I'll sound the alarm, you lock the bloody door quick,' said the other.

A short while later, the door was unlocked and this time two men rushed in and before Clarice knew what was happening they wrapped her in a straitjacket.

Sadie sighed as Clarice was hauled away. She knew where the killer was headed now, somewhere far worse than the prison – the asylum. She watched as the body was removed and the cell cleaned. 'I need a new bucket, don't forget,' she called out as the door was locked again.

Clarice screamed and wriggled but the straitjacket held her fast. 'Where are you taking me?'

'You, lady, are coming with us – to the nuthouse,' one of the men said with a grin.

'Yeah, and we'll have none of your nonsense in there,' said the other as he pinched her cheeks and gave her a sloppy kiss.

'Get off me!' Clarice yelled and kicked the man on the shin.

'You bitch! Get her in the carriage, Stan. Before we get back, this bugger is going to please me, that's for sure!'

Clarice was thrown in the carriage and the door at the back was closed. Stan took up the horse's reins and they set off at walking pace.

Looking at Clarice, the man said, 'If I release you, will you behave?'

'Yes, please take this thing off me.'

The jacket removed, Clarice stared at the man as she rubbed life back into her arms.

'Now then,' he said as he lunged at her. She screamed her lungs out and fought for all she was worth, but the man was stronger and he did indeed take his pleasure. 'I love the ones who fight!' he said as his body shuddered and he moved away from her to button up his trousers. Seeing the blood covering Clarice's thighs, he grinned evilly. 'A virgin! Now weren't I the lucky one!' The man banged on the carriage wall and it was drawn to a halt. The men changed places and Stan took his turn with the woman they were transporting to their place of work. Clarice had no more fight in her and just lay still as she tried to block out what was happening to her. *Despite what I've done, I don't bloody deserve this!* Clarice thought as Stan heaved on top of her. Suddenly her senses returned; there had to be a way out of this!

When he was about to finish, Clarice's hand moved around the carriage floor in search of something that might help. It rested on the straitjacket that had been removed not long before.

Grasping it, she felt the strap and wrapping it around his neck, she pulled as tight as she could.

Stan floundered, trying to get his fingers between the strap and his neck but to no avail, it was so tight it was cutting into his flesh. He lashed out, trying to hit Clarice, but the more he struggled, the tighter she pulled and he let out a sound like a cat being sick. He caught her with a fist and Clarice saw stars but with a knee in his belly now she gritted her teeth and held on for dear life.

It took all of her strength but when she felt his struggles cease, instead of letting go, she pulled tighter still, the weight of his body on her knees heavy. Only when she was certain he was dead did she relax and push him off her. She checked his pulse and found none. Gasping, she wondered where she had found the strength from to defeat this man but guessed adrenaline and survival instinct could account for it. Certainly she had no intentions of going to the asylum and this had proved her only opportunity to prevent that from happening.

Adjusting her clothes, Clarice quickly searched the man's pockets and, finding the key, she opened the back door of the carriage and quietly slipped to the ground. In an instant she was off, running for her life, disappearing into the night like a wraith. She was free and she didn't intend to get caught again, even if it meant living in the shadows with the down and outs.

The carriage rolled on, the driver oblivious to the fact he no longer had an inmate, and his partner was lying dead a few feet behind him.

Darting from shadow to shadow, Clarice made her way through the dark streets. She crept into a garden where some washing had been left out to dry. Taking the shirt, trousers and scarf, she fled the scene. Only when she reached the heathland did she stop to change clothes. The stolen items were damp and cold, but she didn't care. Wrapping the scarf around her head, she hid her prison garb behind a bush and soldiered on. She had to get back to Birmingham to the boarding house where she might be lucky enough to reclaim her things.

As dawn began to break, Clarice walked steadily onwards but realised she'd been away from Birmingham for too long and her things would almost certainly be lost to her, probably sold on by the boarding house owner.

So why was she returning to Birmingham when her plan had been to leave all along? *Maybe the police will be on the lookout for me there!*

Eventually she saw some houses in the distance. Once she knew where she was, she could decide which way to go. As she neared the village, she spotted a sign which said Wolverhampton. That's where she would go! No one would think to look for her there. So off she went in the direction of the town which would let her hide amongst the crowds.

Two days of travelling only at night and hiding where she could in the daytime brought her into the town and she wandered around. She was half starved, having survived on bits of food she had been able to steal or scavenge. Clarice found herself amid a small community of drunks down by the railway line. She knew this could be her home from now on as she was welcomed warmly by those too inebriated to realise she wasn't one of their own.

* * *

Rose had spent a lot of time with Alice over the last few days and they had become quite close. Alice felt Rose was the daughter she never had. It made more sense than both being alone and Alice needed the support now the day of the funeral was at hand.

Jared had broken the sad news to Seth who had cried and sobbed. Then he had run round to Ivy Lane where he and Alice had cried some more.

'He was like a father to me,' Seth had blubbered.

'I know, lad. He thought of both you and Jared as his sons,' Alice had responded.

Jared had taken Alice to select a funeral package and flowers and now he was at her house to escort her to lay her man to rest. Alice had decided against a wake, saying she didn't think she could face it. Besides, she'd told Jared, she wasn't spending hard-earned money on feeding some of the wealthiest people of Birmingham who would undoubtedly attend. She had to get used to living alone and after the interment was as good a time as any to start.

As with Mrs Jenkins's funeral, which seemed so recent still, everyone walked slowly behind the funereal carriage to the church. With Seth one side of Alice and Jared the other, the service proceeded smoothly but once they were out in the cemetery, the situation hit Alice like a pole-axe. The sound began as a soft moan as the coffin was lowered into the ground, then built to a crescendo the like of which Jared had never heard. Her howl rang across the graveyard and then her legs gave way. On her knees, she clawed at the ground and wailed as if to drive away her grief.

Jared and Seth sprang into action and lifted Alice to her feet, but her legs would not support her.

'Fetch a cab, quick!' Jared whispered to Seth. With a nod to the vicar, Jared scooped Alice up into his strong arms and with

Rose by his side, he walked away to the waiting cab. The crowd of mourners all dressed in black began to shuffle their feet and mutter to each other as they watched Jared carry Alice away.

Seth accompanied them to Ivy Lane and, taking the key from Alice, he let them in. He paid the cabbie as Jared again carried Alice indoors and sat her on a kitchen chair. Then Seth came in and busied himself making tea.

'I'm so sorry, Jared,' Alice mumbled.

'Don't worry about a thing, Alice, all will be well in time,' Jared responded.

'I'm going to stay here tonight,' Seth said as he scooched down in front of her.

'You're a good lad. I'll feel better knowing you're here with me.'

'I ain't much of a cook but I can rustle summat up for us,' he said with a grin.

'All right, lovey.' Alice allowed Seth to take over and she sat back, feeling exhausted.

'We'll get off now that we know you're in safe hands,' Jared said and, hugging Alice, he and Rose left for home.

'Now then, missus, what shall we have for tea?' Seth asked.

'There's a pie can be warmed up, we can have that.' Alice's voice was flat and held no enthusiasm.

Over the next few hours, Seth and Alice reminisced with laughter and tears. Seth reminded Alice about how he first met Jared and had accosted him on the street, accusing him of poaching Toby's patch. Then how Jared had had the gall to walk into the yard and hold his hands up; Toby instantly taking a liking to the lad and offering him a job on the spot.

Alice smiled at the memory and told Seth how she had longed to be Toby's wife over many years but he had wanted to build up his business first, consequently Alice had married another. They had, however, enjoyed five years of married bliss, although naturally it was not nearly long enough for Alice.

'Where you going to live once you're wed, Seth?' Alice asked quite suddenly.

Seth explained about renting Rose's family home and Alice asked, 'Why don't you both come here to live with me?'

'What?'

'In return for keeping me company and safe, I'll not charge you a penny in rent. I know Toby left me this house, but I can't face the idea of living here on my own.'

'Alice, are you sure?'

'I am, lad, but how will your Judith react to the offer?'

'There's only one way to find out,' Seth said. 'I'll nip round in the morning and ask her. Jared will understand if I'm a bit late for work.'

That night, Seth heard Alice weeping again and he knocked on her bedroom door, tea in hand. 'Come on, drink this, it might help,' he said when she bade him enter.

'Ta, lad.'

They spent the rest of the night wrapped in blankets on Alice's bed, chatting through their happy memories of Toby.

The following morning, after a bite of breakfast, Seth raced round to the Unicorn. After relating Alice's offer to his fiancée, he asked, 'What do you reckon?'

'You'd be fools not to take her up on it,' Joe put in.

'I agree, Dad,' Judith said, 'but would Rose be offended?'

'I doubt it, she could always rent to someone else. She won't miss out that way,' Seth replied sensibly.

'Fair enough. I'll come back with you to tell Alice that we'll accept her kind offer. You could move in straight away so she's not alone in the meantime.'

The couple made their way over to Ivy Lane and Alice welcomed them in. She was delighted when they told her and Seth thought he saw a spark of the old Alice in her eye. He knew then that they'd made the right decision.

47

'Seth?' Jared said when he answered the knock to the door. 'What's happened? Come in out of the cold.'

Seth greeted Rose before he told them why he was not yet at work.

'I'm sorry, Rose, but it seemed to make sense for me, then Judith, to move in with Alice.'

'It does, Seth, I totally agree. I can soon rent the house out, so don't worry yourself on that score.'

'Look, Seth, take today off too and see to getting yourself settled in with Alice,' Jared said. 'I don't want her on her own any more than is necessary.'

'Thanks, Boss,' Seth said, before shooting off to do just that.

'Bloody hell, what a honeymoon this has turned out to be. I'm sorry, Rose,' Jared said.

'Oh, sweetheart, it couldn't be helped. We're together and that's all that matters.'

Just then there was another knock on the door and Jared cursed. 'We're not gonna get any peace today, I can see.' Answering, Jared invited the man in and introduced him to Rose.

John Connaught looked like he hadn't slept in an age. His pallor was grey and his eyes were surrounded by dark circles. His body slumped in his clothes, which were badly in need of a wash and press. He looked like the walking dead.

Rose made a fresh brew as John took a seat. She offered some cake, unsure of when the man had last eaten. He accepted with a forced smile.

Jared explained to Rose who this man was and how they had come to meet.

'You two fought?' Rose asked with astonishment.

'Not exactly, Mrs Johnson, I charged at Jared and missed; banged my head on the gate post and went down like a ton of bricks,' John answered.

'It turned out Clarice was spreading lies and malicious rumours about her father and that night I met you for the first time she snubbed me in the queue outside the Palace. She pretended not to know me.'

'I see.' Rose poured the tea and cut the cake, placing it before John, who nodded his thanks.

'Jared, if you haven't heard already, I thought you should know. You were her knight in shining armour that day after all despite how she treated you afterwards. Anyway, Clarice has gone to prison.'

Jared's draw dropped open in shock. 'What for?' he managed after a moment.

'Arson and murder.'

'Dear God!' Rose whispered.

'Those fires at the casinos were started by her, and one of them killed a young woman. Clarice was sentenced to life yesterday.' John could no longer hold back his tears and wept openly.

Rose and Jared exchanged a sad look before Jared said, 'I'm sorry to hear that, John.'

Pulling his emotions under control with great effort, John nodded. 'I was at the court. They had shaved her head and dressed her in a prison frock. She looked so lost and forlorn – I could do nothing to help her. I don't even think she knew I was there.'

'I don't know what to say other than that I really am sorry.'

'Thanks, Jared. I'll be on my way now you know. Oh, and congratulations on your wedding.'

'How did you...?' Jared began.

'The two big guys at the yard told me. When I explained why I wanted to see you, they pointed me in this direction.' Turning to Rose, he went on. 'Thank you for the tea, Mrs Johnson, and my apologies for intruding on your happiness.'

'Please think on it no more. Will you be all right?' Rose asked, still thrilled every time she heard her new name.

'Yes. Life goes on, although it will be hard. I don't know if I'll be allowed to visit Clarice in prison or even if she'd want me to, it's something I'll have to enquire about.' Thanking Jared, John Connaught left them and went on his weary way.

'I think we should lock the door and pretend we're not in,' Jared said after a moment.

'It has been a busy few weeks and no mistake,' Rose agreed.

'Do you think we might get a bit of peace now?'

'I wouldn't bank on it,' Rose replied with a smile.

* * *

Clarice guessed it to be about twenty miles to Birmingham, a long way to walk if she decided to try it. As welcome as she had been made by the homeless community, she knew she could not stay in Wolverhampton. Somehow she had to try to find the one person in the world who might show some compassion and help her.

Someone had given her an old jacket and another had provided her with a flat cap. Looking for all the world like a man, Clarice felt she might just manage to get away with the disguise, provided she didn't speak. A woman's voice would give the game away in an instant and folk would wonder why she was dressed in a man's garb.

Hands in trouser pockets, Clarice began her hike back to Birmingham. She had to be extra vigilant and keep her head down so as to not be recognised by anyone who might have known her in either of her previous guises – Clarice or Clara.

Clarice took the heath rather than the roadway, considering it to be the safer option. She thought that the police would be fully aware of what had happened on her journey to the asylum by now and on the lookout for the escapee. They would, however, be searching for a woman.

She walked at a steady pace so as to not tire herself out; she had to reach the city before nightfall. The darkness would help provide cover but she could easily get lost.

Thinking about what had befallen her since she had been banned from the casinos, Clarice regretted the fires she'd set and the death of the woman. The warder who had tried to rape her and the asylum worker she had strangled to death she felt deserved all they got. She was only sorry she hadn't been able to murder the other one as well for what he had done to her.

The sky turned an eerie yellow colour and Clarice thought that more snow could be on the way so she picked up her pace.

On her travels she met only one carter who passed her in the other direction. Nodding in answer to his greeting, she trudged on. The light was failing as she approached her destination. Tired and hungry, Clarice made her way to the place where she would wait. Finding the deepest shadow possible, Clarice stared at the people coming and going from the Grand Theatre, the place Clifford St John loved to visit. He was her only hope now and she had no idea whether he even attended any more. How many nights would she have to wait before she saw him, and more to the point would he be alone?

Her stomach rumbled loudly, begging to be fed, but with no money she couldn't buy food. The best she could do would be to scavenge the market once the theatre had closed. Maybe she would find something which had been discarded that would keep her hunger at bay a while longer.

Clarice watched and waited but there was no sign of Clifford. Then, as she began to turn away, she saw him. He was about to climb into a cab; she had to act now.

Rushing across the road, she said quietly, 'Clifford.'

Turning to face the voice who had called his name, he gasped at the sight of her. 'Clara?'

She nodded. 'Please, Clifford, can you help me?'

His mouth opened and closed like a fish out of water then he said, 'Get in the cab quickly before you are seen!'

With a sigh of relief, Clarice did as she was told.

48

As the cab rolled away, Clifford said, 'I read in the paper that you had been sent to prison!'

'I was, but when I killed a warden for trying to force her attentions on me, they sent for the asylum attendants.'

'Good God! How did you get away?'

Sobs punctuated her explanation of the rapes and how she'd murdered one of the men. She told him how she had walked from Stafford to Wolverhampton and then on to Birmingham to search for him. 'I prayed I might find you.'

'I almost didn't go to the theatre tonight as Anthony cancelled at the last moment. He is unwell.'

'Clifford, I'm sorry but I had no one else to turn to.'

'You know what you did was very wrong, you caused the death of a young woman.'

'I know and I'm sorry for that,' Clarice answered truthfully.

'By rights I should hand you over to the police,' Clifford said.

'Please, Clifford! Please don't, I couldn't bear it if you turned against me too!' Clarice sobbed.

'Oh, my dear girl, you have had such an awful time of it.'

'I have to stay hidden; I mustn't be found, otherwise I will end up in the asylum for sure!'

'That won't happen, you're coming home with me. I'll take care of you.'

'Thank you, Clifford, I know I don't deserve such kindness.'

'Oh, Clara, I've missed you so very much!'

Arriving at Clifford's abode, he paid the cabbie and they walked up the driveway. The house was large and stood in its own grounds, as could be seen in the light of the moon.

'The servants will be in bed, so be quiet. I'll take you up to my room then while you wash I'll find you something to eat and make you a hot drink.'

They tip-toed upstairs and once in the bedroom, Clarice finally relaxed. The gas lamp was lit in readiness for Clifford's return and he gasped again as he took in her appearance.

'My dear, dear girl!'

Clarice's tears fell again as he took her in his arms. 'You're safe now, my darling.'

Clifford went to the kitchen and Clarice stripped and washed from the jug of water on the wash stand. Dressed in one of his shirts she found in the wardrobe, she sat on the bed.

Returning with hot tea and a plate of sandwiches, he smiled. 'You look much better now, although I'm not sure I like the new haircut.'

Clarice managed a smile as she took the refreshments and began to tuck in hungrily.

'Look, I've been thinking. The only way you will be truly safe is if you go abroad.'

'I have nothing, Clifford, I don't even have my own clothes!' she said, spreading her arms.

'I've thought about that too. Tomorrow I'll give the staff the day off. Then I'll go out and buy you some new attire. While I'm out, I will book a passage on a ship bound for the Americas. How does that sound?'

'I... thank you, although I don't know what I'll do out there all alone.'

'Oh, sweetheart, you won't be going on your own – I'll be coming with you,' Clifford said with a cheeky grin.

'Clifford, you can't give up your life here for me!'

'Clara, my life here has been nothing without you! Come away with me, we can start a new life together.'

Clarice nodded, too astounded to answer.

'You're going to need a wig too, I'm thinking.'

For the first time in weeks, Clarice laughed.

The next morning, Clifford, as promised, gave his staff the day off which allowed Clarice to roam around the house unimpeded. He set off in a cab to purchase the items which would be needed for their journey, dresses, ladies' underwear, hats and an outdoor coat plus a dark wig.

He also booked a passage for them both to New York on the first available ship heading out of Liverpool, along with two train tickets to the port. Finally, he had visited the bank to ensure enough money was in the housekeeping account so that his staff would be looked after.

On his return, Clarice excitedly opened the packages as he packed clothes of his own. Then he sat to write explanatory letters to his parents as well as his friend, Anthony.

To Anthony he explained that his heart could not mend without Clara and he had decided to move abroad for a while in the hope of finding a suitable wife. His parents were told much the same thing; but that he had suffered a broken heart and a fresh start was needed. The letters were left on the silver tray in the hall where the maid would find them and post them on his behalf. There also he left a note for his staff saying he would be away for some time, and to keep the house running; the money in the account would see them taken care of for some considerable time. He did this, not only for the staff, but also to enable him to return if things went sideways with Clarice out in America.

Clarice appeared dressed, wig in place and hat pinned to it, and Clifford's heart sang. 'Oh, my love, there you are and looking radiant.'

'Thank you, Clifford,' Clarice said, giving him a twirl.

'We catch the last train out of New Street to Liverpool where we board ship to New York,' he informed her. 'We'll travel in the darkness to ensure we are not seen.'

Clarice ran to him and, falling to her knees, she began to cry.

'Darling, what's this?' Clifford asked, full of concern.

'Clifford, I don't deserve any of it. I've killed people and I know I should be punished for that, but it was so horrid what they did to me!'

'I know, my sweet, and that's why I'm taking you away from here. Now dry your eyes.' He passed her his handkerchief, then with a grin he added. 'In New York there are countless casinos, so you can play cards as much as you want.'

'Oh, Clifford!' Clarice flung her arms around him, deliriously happy at the thought.

Later that night, a cab took them to the station where a train bore them to Liverpool. Under cover of darkness, they boarded a ship which would carry them across the ocean, and Clarice revelled in her freedom and the knowledge she would be able to gamble once more before too long.

Clifford was still unsure whether he could trust Clara again but his love for her was so strong he was willing to give it a try.

* * *

Jared returned to work and before long Alice had received a letter from the probate office saying she could access Toby's estate. The inheritances were paid out by the bank following the instructions of the solicitor and Seth was back in his old room at Ivy Lane.

Judith, with help from Rose and Alice, was preparing for her wedding and the lads were looking forward to another good knees-up.

The newspapers were full of the story of the murderess who was still at large, with every police force far and wide on the lookout for her. Of course, she wouldn't be found, for she and her paramour were now aboard a ship bound for America.

Clarice had adopted the name of Clara Worthington and had promised Clifford faithfully that she would treat him with more respect in the future. She had admitted to her abominable behaviour and had vowed her loyalty to him. Clifford had forgiven her because he loved her more than words could say. He suggested when they landed perhaps they should be married. He almost jumped for joy when Clarice agreed.

On the day of Seth and Judith's wedding, Jared, as best man, stood with a very nervous bridegroom in the church, awaiting the arrival of his bride-to-be.

'Oh, Jared, she's late! What if she doesn't come?'

'Seth, we're early. There's plenty of time and she *will* come. She wouldn't buy a wedding gown to then not turn up now, would she?'

'I suppose.'

'I know how you feel, I was the same.'

Seth turned for the thousandth time and then he saw his mum enter the church. Jumping to his feet, he rushed to greet her. They hugged each other tightly and he whispered, 'I'm glad you came.'

'I wouldn't have missed it for the world,' Molly Watkins answered. Guided to her place on the front pew by her son, Seth then retook his seat next to Jared, who said hello to Molly with a smile. On Jared's advice, Seth had taken Judith to Dudley to meet his mum and the two women hit it off immediately.

Over at the Unicorn, Joe Whitman was sobbing at the sight of his daughter in her white velvet wedding gown. Nipped in at the waist, it buttoned to the neck at the front, the long sleeves coming to a point on the back of her hands. A veil was held in place by a tiara of white silk roses.

Judith was almost undone seeing her dad cry.

'Oh, Judy, you look beautiful and so much like your mum.'

With a smile, she said, 'Come on, I don't want to be late otherwise we'll have Seth banging on the door.'

With a nod and a grin, Joe led his girl, who carried a small prayer book, out to the waiting cab.

When the bride and her father arrived at the church, they stood in the doorway where the vicar spotted them.

The vicar's fingers wiggled, calling Seth and Jared to their feet, and the organ suddenly increased in pitch.

The two friends turned to watch Judith sail down the aisle on the arm of her father. Jared caught sight of a tear rolling down Seth's cheek and he grinned. He knew just how his pal was feeling.

The vicar started by welcoming everyone into his church and then the service proper began. There was silence as the words rang out clear as a bell. Then it came to the vows.

'I, Seth Watkins, take thee, Judith Kingston...' Seth repeated after the vicar as he looked into his beloved's eyes.

Judith kept her eyes on his as she also repeated the vicar's words.

There was an almost audible intake of breath when the vicar

asked the question finishing with 'speak now or forever hold his peace'.

Then he announced, 'I now pronounce you man and wife. You may kiss your...' He stopped short as Seth whipped his arms around Judith and kissed her passionately. '...wife!'

After congratulating the happy couple, everyone retired to the Unicorn to enjoy the wedding breakfast.

Someone had dragged an upright piano into the bar and began playing loudly as the couple entered.

All along one wall, trestle tables had been set up and covered with cloths. Dishes of food were crammed on the tables, leaving barely room for the cutlery. There was game pie, cheeses, ham off the bone, sausages, fresh bread, pork pies, cakes, rice puddings, fruit and bread and butter pudding as well as lots more to tempt the palate. The cook had done a splendid job. Pokey and his friend tended the bar and beer and wine began to flow.

'Only us to find brides now,' Sam said a little sadly to Paul, who stood next to him.

Just then, a bevy of pretty girls came through the door, all giggling and laughing, evidently friends of Judith and her father.

'I say!' Dan said.

'So do I!' Tom added and Paul nodded eagerly.

Johnny was busy at the bar getting the drinks in so it was Sam who strolled over. Showing them to a table, he stayed to chat.

Watching the ladies laugh at something Sam said, the others took a bet on which one Sam would be escorting home.

Jared sat with Rose and Alice and he almost fainted when Rose whispered, 'I think I may be pregnant.'

'How do you know, we've only just been wed ourselves!' Jared said in disbelief.

'Jared, I just know,' Rose said in an exasperated tone. 'But I want to keep it a secret for now. I want us to enjoy this alone before we share our news with everyone.'

'All right, my love,' he answered before giving her a kiss.

The next few weeks saw Seth and Judith settled into the other end of Alice's house. Judith had explained to her father she only wanted to work four days at the Unicorn and wished to be with her new husband as much as possible. Joe had agreed readily, saying she had made the right choice. So Judith, Seth and Alice spent many hours together in the evenings.

Alice mentioned one night that she didn't see much of Jared, Rose and the lads any more and was a little sad about it. She knew they were busy with work and leading their own lives, but she missed their company.

'Why not invite them to dinner sometime?' Judith suggested. 'I'd be happy to help with the cooking.'

'That's a bostin' idea, gel. What about Saturday night?' Alice said as she visibly perked up.

'I'll let them know tomorrow at work then,' Seth said.

'Right now, Judith, what shall we give them to eat?' Alice said.

The next few hours were spent compiling a menu and Seth saw a spark in Alice's eye which had been missing for quite a while.

Judith did all the shopping for their meal and everyone agreed with gusto, looking forward to one of Alice's legendary dinners.

Saturday night saw everyone arrive, some with wine, others with flowers and Alice greeted them with all with warm hugs. Roast beef with all the trimmings was wolfed down, much to Alice's delight. She loved to cook for those who loved to eat.

It was when they were all sitting in the huge living room that Rose gave Jared the nod.

'Firstly I'd like to thank Alice for the wonderful meal.' Applause sounded along with whistles. When the noise died down, he went on, 'Rose and I have something we'd like to share with you. We're going to have a baby.'

Everyone jumped to their feet and shook Jared's hand and clapped him on the back by way of congratulations.

'What's going on?' Tim asked as he returned from the privy.

'You are going to be a granddad,' Jared said with a grin as wide as a mile.

Tim hugged his son and blew a kiss to Rose. She laughed as she caught it and placed her hand on her belly.

When Jared came back to her side, Rose said, 'If it's a boy, can we call him Toby?'

Alice burst into tears as Jared said, 'To be sure.'

ABOUT THE AUTHOR

Lindsey Hutchinson is a bestselling saga author whose novels include *The Workhouse Children*. She was born and raised in Wednesbury, and was always destined to follow in the footsteps of her mother, the multi-million selling Meg Hutchinson.

Sign up to Lindsey Hutchinson's mailing list for news, competitions and updates on future books.

Follow Lindsey on social media:

f facebook.com/Lindsey-Hutchinson-1781901985422852

🐦 twitter.com/LHutchAuthor

BB bookbub.com/authors/lindsey-hutchinson

ALSO BY LINDSEY HUTCHINSON

Sixpence Stories

Introducing Sixpence Stories!

Discover page-turning
historical novels from your
favourite authors, meet new
friends and be transported
back in time.

Join our book club
Facebook group

https://bit.ly/SixpenceGroup

Sign up to our
newsletter

https://bit.ly/SixpenceNews

Boldwood

Boldwood Books is an award-winning fiction publishing company seeking out the best stories from around the world.

Find out more at www.boldwoodbooks.com

Join our reader community for brilliant books, competitions and offers!

Follow us
@BoldwoodBooks
@TheBoldBookClub

Sign up to our weekly deals newsletter

https://bit.ly/BoldwoodBNewsletter